CON

Prologue

2000

Jonty, the night master, was in a stupor when the boy reached into the office to get the front door key off the hook on the wall at the side of the door. A small mound of tobacco and several Rizlas littered the floor around his bare feet, as another attempt to roll a spiff slipped through his trembling nicotine-stained fingers. His whiskey glass empty, his eyes like slits, fought to stay open as he fell back on the couch to snore, grunt and fart his way through the rest of the night.

Outside the air was cool. A light drizzle sprayed the boy's face and he stood for a few seconds to savour it. He'd planned this mission carefully, sat upstairs for hours waiting for everyone to go to sleep, and for Jonty to surrender to his Friday night drugs and booze session. He wondered if anyone else was brave enough to be out at this unholy hour, when according to the horror movies, evil lurked in the shadows and Freddy Krueger-like characters watched your every move.

It was as quiet as a graveyard. A sudden gust of wind whipped the trees on the driveway into a frenzy and a shiver ran down his spine as he imagined demons leaping out to drag him to hell. He pulled the hood of his navy anorak over his head and quickened his pace, afraid to look right or left. If he didn't look, they wouldn't see him.

The house was in darkness when he got there, except for the landing light which she left on to deter burglars and the like. The first of four houses in this quiet cul-de-sac, the detached four bed nineteen-seventies' residence had seen better days.

In the beam of a street lamp it looked shabby compared to the other three. White paint had peeled from the cracked dry woodwork and fallen like snow on to the pathway.

Bushes and creeping vines obscured half of a large bay window and a privet hedge that bordered the overgrown lawn was taller than the garage roof.

It was hard to imagine a well-known surgeon had once lived here. The old man would huff and puff like a Tasmanian Devil if he could see it now. He'd kept the privet trimmed, like the crewcut of an American GI, and shaped in a perfect oblong along the edge of the property, until his death five years ago.

The boy crept round to the back of the house, clocked a galvanized bucket in the corner of his eye and stepped over it. She'd more than likely placed it there to catch someone out, someone like him, who was up to no good. The small kitchen window was open as usual. Her mangy old cat had always been more welcome than he had.

He slipped off his boots. They were new, probably donated to the home by some well-meaning old witch because her husband had dropped down dead before he could wear them out. People were always bringing stuff in for the poor orphans. He rubbed the back of his heel to soothe the itching blister that threatened to burst at any minute.

Tall for his age he climbed up on to the window ledge with ease, then reached in through the small window to open the big one. He edged his way to the inside ledge, careful not to make a noise or knock anything over. Not that she would hear him, she'd be out like a light, ginned up. But the nosey old bag next door had ears like a bat and a nose like a bloodhound. He knew every inch of this house, he'd been dumped here often enough when his parents had been out socializing with their celebrity friends, and it had never been a nice experience. The old woman was as bitter as a lemon. He recalled breakfasts of half cooked, unsweetened porridge oats and hard dry toast that would have your eye out if you threw it like a shuriken.

His hands wandered slowly over the draining board, feeling for plates or cutlery that he might disturb. He wondered if she still had the plastic Humpty Dumpty dish she'd insisted he use for every meal. Her Willow Pattern was much too good for the likes of him. There was nothing there. He closed the window then let himself down softly on to the cold grey tiled floor and waited while his eyes focused in the dark.

The cooker to his right, then oak cupboards topped with beige work surfaces. To his left a table and two chairs, next to them the fridge freezer. It hadn't changed a bit in the two years since he was here. Outdated wasn't the word, it was almost antique. The old woman had always been stingy, even though she had thousands in the bank, and the house had not been decorated since she and her husband moved in over twenty-five years ago.

The stairs creaked. He stood stock still to listen, his heart pounded wildly in his chest and a bead of sweat ran down his cheek. Suddenly the kitchen door flung open and she stood in the beam of light that shone into the hallway from the street lamp at the front of the house.

'Who's there?' she demanded. She held a shoe at shoulder height.

He moved closer to her, so she could see him in the beam, and grinned. 'You really shouldn't keep leaving the window open, old woman. You never know who's prowling about these days. That shoe would just about kill a spider.'

Fear registered in her small, dark eyes and her eyebrows jumped two inches up her brow to hide in greasy grey curls. She stepped back.

'It's you! What do you want? You shouldn't be here!'

'I've come out especially to see you. I need to thank you for what you did for me.'

'Thank me?' Her voice went up three octaves. 'What are you talking about? I had you put away! Now get out of here! I'm going to call the police!'

Two quick steps across the room and he grabbed

her by the throat. 'Oh no, you're not! I'm going to show you what it's like when you cry for help and no-one wants to hear you.' He closed the door with his foot and dragged her to the middle of the room. The old woman struggled, she dropped the shoe and bit the gloved hand he had across her mouth.

'Fucking bitch!'

In a split second he had her on the floor, grabbed her hair and banged her head on the hard tiles. Three heavy clouts, the last one cracked her skull with a sickening crunch, her eyes rolled back and she gasped. Blood spread across the floor like a pool of black tar. Her body twitched and writhed. It reminded him of a mouse he caught in the garden at the children's home. Its legs were still moving a minute after he cut the head off.

He was on top of her and could feel the heat of her body around his groin. Her breath smelled of gin, her pink floral nightdress reeked of lavender water as he lifted it and put his hand inside her pants.

'You're going to like this,' he whispered close to her ear.

A loud groan escaped from her throat and she frothed at the mouth as he raped her.

Beads of sweat dripped off the end of his nose on to her face and neck.

'That's the best shag I've ever had. Well, it's the only shag I've ever had,' he laughed. He stood up and listened for any sign that someone might have heard him.

The kitchen clock ticked loudly. Another groan

escaped from the old woman's throat and startled him. 'Fucking bitch!' He kicked her twice.

It was time to go. He unlocked the back door, fetched a can of petrol from the shed, doused her body with it, scattered a few matches over her, then placed the open box near her hand. She was still breathing. That was good. He wanted her to feel pain. He took a few matches with him to the back door, wiped the floor with a tea towel and put it in his coat pocket. He quickly put his boots back on, wincing as one of the blisters on his heel popped, struck a match on the step, threw it in and closed the door. Through the small window in the door he saw the ball of flames, turned and ran.

When he got back Jonty was still asleep on the old brown leather couch in the office. His ginger hair looked like a ball of tumbleweed on the red cushion and one arm hung and touched the floor. The bastard looked like a dead body. The smell of weed and whiskey hung in the air. The boy knew this man hated him.

'Your time will come,' he whispered, as he slipped the key back on the hook and went to bed.

Chapter One

2013

She was alone in this dark dingy room full of spiders and moths and other crawling insects. When he first carried her up here, she could still see and walk a little. She didn't know how long ago that was. It seemed like forever now. She'd looked for a way out but had stumbled and fell over the bucket he'd left for her to use as a toilet.

The pain in the side of her head where he hit her with a hammer made her feel dizzy and sick, so she lay curled up on a blood-stained mattress in the corner of the room, eyes closed, silent and still. She looked like a pile of old clothes you'd throw out for the rag and bone man.

It was a room where the door had been covered with the same paper as the wall. A gold flock-type paper that was soft to touch. At least she thought it was. Her mind had become cloudy and confused. She knew posh people had rooms like this. She'd seen it on television, 'Through the Keyhole'. Was it Elton John or Lord and Lady Muck who had a house like this?

What did it matter? It was her prison. She thought all rich folk were stuck up. Who would paper the door the same as the walls and take away the door handle, but an idiot or a madman? He was a madman, a raving lunatic.

The smell of death, mould and body waste was so strong it choked her. She knew it was death. She just couldn't understand why. She wasn't a bad person.

She'd been a bit promiscuous, taken a few drugs, smoked weed, but surely she didn't deserve this? There were people out there who murdered, raped and robbed. Why did it have to be her who lay here, rotting in her own shit? What had she done to be treated in such an inhuman way?

She knew he watched her at this very moment. His evil presence leaked into the room, like a laser beam, through the peephole he'd made in the door. He always watched her. He watched her dress, sleep, eat and wash. Now he watched her die.

She hadn't the strength to get upset about it anymore.

When he brought her to the house he treated her like a princess. She could ask for anything and he'd provide it. Clothes, food, DVDs and make-up. He said he locked her in the room for her own protection and she believed him. But as the weeks passed he became more demanding and ordered her to dance or sing or strip naked. She was willing to do anything at first, because he'd saved her. Then he became violent and punched her if she showed any reluctance to do as he said. He drugged her and tied her to the bed to do his vile, disgusting experiments.

Why did she go with him? Why wouldn't she? She already knew him from the hospital where they met. It had been a long, close friendship. He seemed a quiet, gentle soul, the kind of boy any parent would want their daughter to marry. She thought she would be safe with him. Safe? My god! She couldn't have been more wrong.

A dark cloud formed in her mind. It pushed out more of her thoughts. Her space was getting smaller. Soon there would be no room for her thoughts and she would drift into oblivion. She could see herself at ten years old and it was Christmas. The tree was laden with baubles and bright flashing lights, the smell of stuffing and mince pies filled the room. Her father laughed and teased her, a twinkle in his eye.

'What bicycle are you talking about?'

'Oh, Daddy! You promised, Daddy. Didn't he promise, Mommy?'

'Wait and see, darling,' her mother replied as she tried to repress a smile.

The image vanished as quickly as it had appeared. She was back in that place between life and nothing, a grey area with occasional bursts of light. She couldn't open her eyes anymore, the effort was too great. Hunger and thirst had abandoned her, given up on her, as if they too knew it was too late. She thought if she could get up and walk round she might feel better, but she couldn't move. She tried to concentrate to move just one finger, but her mind floated, like the clouds, or a ship on a stormy sea, it veered from one thought to another, as if she flicked through the pages of her life story.

Something was in the room. She heard it crunch

on her feet bones. It had fed on her for days. At first it was painful, now she couldn't feel her feet or any part of her body. How much of her had it eaten? It was a rat, or maybe two rats. 'Oh, my god! What did I do to deserve this?' Her voice screamed in her head. 'I'm only twenty-three!'

Why had she left home? Her parents had been good to her, they'd saved every penny for her last operation. Her father had done untold overtime at the glassworks, her mother had worn her fingers to the bone doing clothes alterations on her old Singer sewing machine. If she hadn't gone with Rick, who promised her the earth, she wouldn't be here now. Maybe she wouldn't have gone with he who watched.

Rick got her hooked on drugs, then slung her aside like an old shoe. He, who watched, came at just the right time to save her. To save her? He did things to her that no other human would even think of. She was strung up like a joint of meat and had objects pushed into her vagina and anus. He used metal operating clamps to open her vagina so that he could put other things in, like mice and spiders and god knows what else. He stood there and laughed as she writhed in agony. The more she screamed, the more excited he became and he turned up his death music and waved his arms around like a mad conductor.

Then he began the operations. He cut warts and moles off her arms and back without an anaesthetic. He called this torture 'experiments of human endurance' and wrote pages of how she reacted to the pain and every word she uttered.

The dark cloud had invaded every corner of her mind. There was only a little bit of space left now.

Thoughts popped into her head as if she pulled them randomly from a conjuror's hat. Mother sat at her sewing machine and chewed her nails as she studied a complicated dress pattern. Grandma made tea. The teaspoon rattled loudly on the cup. Grandma couldn't hear the racket she made, she was deaf. Father tinkered with his car and cursed when the spanner slipped. They all vanished into thin air, like a mirage in the desert.

Something buzzed near her ear. The flies. They were here to lay eggs in her rotting flesh. Soon maggots would eat her. 'Oh, please God! Somebody save me! Take me out of this!' Her silent voice screamed.

The doctor who fixed her leg when she was a child was so nice. 'Here's a lollipop, you've been such a brave girl.' He smiled at her, but then his face became contorted like a swimming mass of skin and morphed into he who watched.

'God help me!' Her final plea, as the dark cloud spread to every corner of her mind and left nothing but death to claim her last memory.

Her eyes flickered and her mouth dropped open as she took a final breath.

Suddenly there was sunshine and birdsong. She sat on a blanket in the garden. There were beautiful flowers, daffodils, roses and tulips, the splatter of water from the ornamental fountain and happy people. She was home.

'Come on baby, walk to Grandma.' Her grandmother stood in front of her holding out her arms. 'Come on sweetie, you can do it.'

'I'm coming, Grandma! I'm coming now!'

Chapter Two

He carefully prepared the room for the next guest. The walls and ceiling shone with a fresh coat of white paint. The bed, cupboard, sink, toilet, all white, like the walls, as cold as ice. His pale bloodless fingers worked diligently, as they covered cracks in the wall and smoothed the white bed sheet like spiders walking on snow.

The floor, large grey quarry tiles, that had been there for over a hundred years, was scrubbed free of the blood that spattered when he cracked her skull with the hammer.

A small window above the sink was screwed shut from the outside, with panes painted white to hide secrets and misdeeds that no-one should see. He wondered what his father would think of him, now he was master of the house. Everything was ready. All he had to do was pick up his guest.

He looked through the peephole in the door. The bed was in line with it, so that he could watch whoever was in there. A strong ripple of excitement turned his stomach over. It wouldn't be long now.

On the outside of this rundown country residence, padlocked wooden shutters on the windows blocked out the sun's intrusive rays and other unwelcome visitors.

Blistered white paint fell from window frames, to reveal dry cracked woodwork, like lines on an old man's face. Tall conifers guarded the edge of the property like sentinels, and padlocked rusty iron gates blocked the driveway from anyone wishing to enter.

In the walled garden a decorative stone pathway had sunk beneath a sea of thick, green moss and once thriving roses, daffodils and hyacinths were trapped and choked in a tangle of chickweed, nettles and dandelions. A haven for frogs, snails and other slimy creatures.

This dark lonely place was three miles from the nearest town. No whistling postman, nor cheery milkman walked its pathway. No-one knew who or what was behind these walls, no-one could hear the bloodcurdling screams that emanated from locked doors and travelled long, dark corridors, as they tried to find a way to freedom or an ear to listen to their story. To those who passed by it looked like it had been abandoned to rot many years ago. A wooden sign on the gate declared 'TRESPASSERS WILL BE PROSECUTED'. No-one had trespassed. A faded brass sign on the wall read 'Tipley Manor House'.

As a boy he played in the corridors of this spacious home. He knew every corner and niche where the monster couldn't find him. As he slid the three bolts across to lock the door he shook as he recalled the nights his father would come to his room to punish him for wrongdoing.

There was always something he had done that displeased his father. There was always a reason for the punishment. He might have pulled a face at the food he was given, or laughed at the wrong time, or forgotten to say thank you for being born.

He was guilty without being tried and it was futile to argue, that only made his father more angry. So he came to accept what his father said he had done and take the punishment he was given. He blocked out the pain, while his heart became a stone and he plotted his revenge.

He knew the reason for the punishment was his deformed left leg and foot.

His father could barely look at him and regarded him as something grotesque. With his film star pose, dark brown hair and penetrating smoky blue eyes, he was a Pierce Brosnan lookalike. He was also a perfectionist, he was obsessive in his work and in his life and was mortified when his son was born with a deformity. The doctors called it 'Tibial Hemimelia' and discussed the long process of bone treatment for his leg, foot and knee.

The news devastated him. As one of the most outstanding plastic surgeons in the country, he'd published papers on his work and his ideas to improve established procedures. He was the star for the stars, his client list read more like a cast list for a Hollywood movie. He was a cosmetic surgeon, he made ugly people beautiful, or beautiful people more beautiful and was deeply ashamed of producing a child who was not perfect in every way, a child he hid away from the public and his clients.

After years of operations and wearing distraction apparatus on his leg and foot the boy still had a pronounced limp and his left foot was smaller than his right one. His father continued to ridicule and mock him and made him wear the 'special shoe' with the huge sole. A nanny was hired to look after him throughout his early childhood, but as soon as he could feed and dress himself she was dismissed and the boy lost the only love he would ever know.

He didn't go to school, he was taught at home by a tutor who despised him for his deformity and his intelligence. His mother rarely visited him in the nursery, his father came only to punish him for imagined wrongdoing. They dutifully showed up for his treatment at a private clinic when their signatures were required for his operations.

Few people knew the boy existed. He spent his days reading in the nursery, or skulking about the house, trying to keep out of his father's way, when he was there, and watching his mother drink herself into unconsciousness.

After his last meal he was confined to his room. If he was caught disobeying this rule he was beaten by his father. He sneaked out when he knew it was safe, when they were busy doing things in the cellar.

Chapter Three

He parked in the shade of oak trees that lined the wide road. Their huge tangled roots had lifted paving slabs and made part of the walkway unsafe for pedestrians. A cardboard sign pinned to one of them read 'SAVE OUR TREES'. Planted over sixty years ago they were a striking feature on both sides of this long road. He was happy they were there, not because he was a lover of nature, he didn't care if they were chopped down tomorrow but the overhanging leafy branches were a useful cover for what he was about to do.

He looked up and down the road. No-one coming his way. This was going to be easy. He checked his watch. Five minutes to go. Today he was the Doctor but he wasn't visiting the sick, the one foot in the grave folk or some useless new mother, he was on a mission to find a bride.

This was one of the nicer areas of Dudstone, with the college, library and council offices a mile up the road on the edge of the town centre, and a few yards further in the centre, the local police station. The huge detached houses to his left housed the elite of the town, judges, solicitors, doctors, the mayor. They lay far back from the road and each boasted landscaped gardens and decorative wrought iron gates.

In the north west corner of the park lay the priory ruins, known locally for the haunting of the headless nun, stories of illicit love and murdered babies that were buried in the cellars. To the north east lay the tennis courts, and in the middle the pond and play area.

Standing on a hill above the park, Dudstone Castle overlooked the town like a beacon and reminded the inhabitants of the many famous Norman kings, dukes, earls and lords who had once ruled over them with a rod of iron. On the other side of the wide road stood a row of linked town houses, a few shops and behind them the other half of Castle council estate, which had been built in the mid-nineteen-thirties to house tenants from slum areas of the town that were demolished. The laundry was closed now and the newsagents would be closing in a few minutes. The off license had just opened. It was quiet this time of the day as people wound down for the weekend. To his left, next to the last large house, an expanse of green bordered the park, where in the distance mothers and children played by the pool, too far away to notice him.

He knew this area well. The house he'd bought was just two streets away, next to the college. It was a detached residence with a small concrete garden and a garage.

Here he could be whoever he wanted to be. He played a number of characters, all of whom worked together to achieve his goals. He rarely saw any neighbours except for the occasional nod or 'good morning' and was quiet in his comings and goings. Few people knew him, mainly those he worked with, but none were allowed into his private life. For now his name was Michael, or maybe Philip.

This was near to the place where he'd kidnapped the last girl. That had sent the local police round in circles. One officer in particular would have loved to meet him, to be here right now, but he was too clever, he was like a shadow, a thief in the night, a now-you-see-me, now-you-don't enigma. Tomorrow he would be someone else. Someone you probably wouldn't give a second glance. He might come to mend the plumbing, or cut the lawn, but in his bag was a scalpel, a hammer and a saw that were hardly used for their intended purpose. In his mind death danced around you, like the lady who shimmered in the lamp at the beginning of *Tales of Mystery and Imagination*, and waited for the right moment to strike.

He watched a mongrel chew on a chip wrapping paper that had been dropped near a litter bin on the path to the park. He turned the radio on. The news again. He was tired of hearing about the new royal baby. Who cared what his name would be? He switched channels. Michael Jackson sang 'The Girl is Mine'.

'Nice day for a kidnapping,' he chuckled, as he cracked the window open, looked in the mirror, adjusted his dark glasses and made sure the red baseball cap covered his short dark hair. He was getting damn good at this! Number three was about to join his household. Sweat from his brow ran down the side of his cheek. He'd be glad when this was over and he had his little princess. The excitement played havoc with his stomach and bladder. He blamed his father for this.

As a child he would shake with fear as he waited for his father to come to his room and the abuse and torture to begin. He felt the agitation rise in his chest and stomach, nausea began to wash over him and he quickly dismissed the thought from his mind.

The nervous tic below his right eye began to twitch. He must concentrate. He couldn't fuck up now.

Another few minutes and she'd be here. She was a creature of habit, and that was her downfall. Some people just didn't realise that their habits were the things that always let them down. They went round in a dream, with no thought that there were people like him who waited for the right moment to cock-up their well-ordered lives.

Fucking idiots! They deserved all they got. It could be all over the TV and newspapers that a murderer was loose, but they still stuck to their stupid routines.

Their philosophy was that it would never happen to them, it always happened to people in other towns, or other countries. Their minds were closed to the fact that there were people like him in every country, every town and every street, who waited for that right moment. Anyone could do exactly what he was about to do. They just had to watch someone they wanted to own, follow them home and wait until they were alone. He believed there was evil in everyone and all it needed was a little mishap to bring it out. He was brilliant at causing mishaps! Jack Riley had almost strangled an innocent man when his little girl had gone missing.

Now this girl, Catherine, deserved what was about to happen to her. She never changed her routine, she always walked home along the same route at the same time every day. For an intelligent girl she was absolutely predicable. She didn't listen to the news, or read the papers, she was far too busy enjoying her youth. She worked until five-thirty on Fridays because the library ran an after school reading club. Most of the other workers round here finished at two.

He glanced at the cloth, chloroform and twine on the back seat, and hoped she wouldn't struggle too much. He didn't want to damage her, she was going to be his bride, his new Rebecca. He had everything ready for the ceremony back at his house.

He remembered the first time he'd seen her as she came out of the library and how he'd deliberately bumped into her.

'I'm so sorry,' she apologised. 'I was miles away.'

He looked into those beautiful blue eyes and knew he had to own her. He was angry with himself after she'd gone for not talking and keeping her there. That's how he was with girls, tongue-tied. They always shunned him and boys always mocked him and called him names. 'Limp wimp!' 'Club foot!'. He could hear them now. But they would all be sorry. They would learn to respect him, just like the girl he already owned.

After that first meeting he wore a disguise whenever he went to the library because he knew it would all be on CCTV. He knew the police would check it when she went missing, but they wouldn't be able to recognise him as he really was. He always wore a dark suit, silver rimmed spectacles and a blond wig. Adding the briefcase gave a good impression he thought, and he looked just like the other office workers who came in to read during their lunch break.

He'd watched her replace the borrowed books and read to the kids in the children's corner, with posters of Winnie the Pooh and SpongeBob all over the wall. She was so graceful, like a swan or a ballerina. She never noticed him in the reading room, up on the balcony, as he looked down on her and pretended to read a newspaper, or sat at a computer terminal just a few yards away from her.

He watched. He waited. Now it was time to act.

She was coming. His heart did a double somersault. He could see her in the distance, her long blond hair lifted slightly in the gentle breeze, as she glided elegantly along the road. The blue cotton dress hugged and highlighted her slender legs and thighs. She looked like an angel descending on a cloud. He was aroused by the sight of her.

Chapter Four

Catherine had been on her feet all day at the library. It was a temporary job for the summer before she began a degree in Humanities at Larchester University. She was tired and wanted to get home and soak in the bath for an hour before she got ready to meet her friends, Leanne and Alice. As she thought about where they were going, her eyes settled on a young man near the entrance to the park, who reached into the open rear door of his car.

It was Alice's eighteenth birthday in three days. A group them were going to celebrate at The Factory, a disco club in town that catered for fourteen- to eighteen-year-olds. Catherine's eighteenth birthday was two weeks away. She'd recently passed her driving test and her parents were buying her a car. She thought about Andy. At lunchtime he'd finally asked her for a date. Butterflies danced in her stomach. Her father wouldn't like her having a boyfriend. She felt sick at the thought of what he would say if he knew she wanted to go out with Andy. Why had she let him spoil her entire life? Why hadn't she told someone about him and what he'd done to her? There were so many people who could help her now. She'd put the phone number for Child Help in her mobile but had been too scared to call it. Maybe she was to blame for what he'd done. He said she was a teaser, but she wondered how an eight-year-old child could be provocative. It was just taking that first step to tell someone. Perhaps if she did the fear and guilt she felt right now might go away. Child abuse. The words sent a shiver through her. She must have done something to make her father do what he did. She must have been a bad girl. What could she do to make things right? If only people knew the torment she suffered every day and the heartache behind her smile.

'You're my special girl, Catherine. Don't tell anyone because they will send you away and you'll never see me and mommy again.' The words had gone through her mind a million times over the years. She didn't want to disappoint her father. Was that it? Was that the reason she hadn't told anyone? What would it have done to her mother if she'd told someone? She loved her mother. That's why she kept the secret.

She wished she could tell one of her friends. One who wouldn't judge her.

Alice and Leanne were good friends, but she'd heard what they said about other girls and knew they would be shocked, disgusted even. She'd pretended for so long now she would be embarrassed to tell them. Her father was a pillar in society, her mother the obedient vicar's wife. How could she tell the people she knew so well the truth, when she'd lived a lie for so long? She was almost an adult and she'd let it go on.

The more it happened, the harder it was to stop, until it became a way of life, secretive and dirty. People wouldn't understand if she told them. They would blame her and call her bad names. The truth was she felt unworthy of being loved by someone nice like Andy. She wasn't sure what to do about him. She wanted to go out with him, but when she thought about her father, all the good feelings Andy gave her floated away like dandelion seeds on a breeze. He would hate her if he knew what she'd done. She hated herself.

Her thoughts were interrupted by loud cheers from a group of people as she neared the path to the park.

He trembled as he opened the car door. 'Stay calm. Stay calm,' he muttered to himself.

Someone screamed and startled him, then a man ran across the road into the park.

He shook from head to toe. This wasn't what he'd planned, it could all go wrong. A small crowd had gathered in the park. The commotion had worked as a convenient distraction from him, but all the shouting and screaming had put him on edge. He looked at the crowd in the park, then back to Catherine, who looked across the park to see what was going on.

People cheered and clapped.

'Hurry! Hurry!' he whispered as she drew closer. 'Please don't go in the park.'

As she passed, he turned, grabbed her, threw her on the back seat and pressed the soaked cloth over her mouth and nose. She struggled and kicked for a few seconds but soon succumbed to the suffocating cloth. He took a plastic bag from his pocket and dropped the handkerchief he had ready on to the footpath. Someone was going to get a nasty shock. He grabbed her bag, closed the door and walked quickly to the driver's side and got in. He took her mobile phone from the bag and switched it off.

As he pulled away he had to brake sharply when a man emerged from the park and ran straight into the road without looking. Then he heard the sirens.

Chapter Five

Detective Inspector Jack Riley had had a long day and was in need of a drink. It started with an armed robbery at a post office in Tipley and finished with a fight outside the Loving Lamb pub in the town centre. He was tired of filling out witness statements and listening to the drunks who'd fought over a local prostitute. He charged them with being drunk and disorderly and locked them in the cells to sober up. The prostitute had denied any involvement, so Jack let her off with a caution.

The off-licence on Broad Street was now open. The whiskey had become a bit of a habit lately but he'd stuck to his resolve of just one double a night and two on Saturdays and Sundays.

When he came out of the off-licence he heard hysterical screams coming from the park across the road. He threw the bottle on the back seat of the car and ran towards the noise. As Jack got closer he could see a heavily pregnant woman who pointed to what looked like a piece of blue cloth floating in the pool. He realised it was a small child and waded into the water, grabbed the child, hurried back and laid him on the grass.

The boy had stopped breathing, his lips were blue. Jack dropped to his knees and gave the boy two gentle breaths of mouth to mouth.

'Has anyone called an ambulance?' he shouted between breaths, as a burst of panic rose in his chest, seconds ticked loudly in his head and the boy showed no signs of life. He moved the boy's arms up and down in a pumping motion, then lifted him up, put him across his knee and slapped his back three times. The child coughed up some water and began to breathe.

Onlookers, who had gathered, cheered and clapped as Jack lifted the shivering boy into his arms and carried him to his distraught mother.

'Thank you. Thank you,' the child's mother sobbed. 'I must have dozed off for a few minutes.'

Jack watched as she stroked and kissed her boy. A bad day had ended with something good He put his hand up to her and trotted back towards his car, as the siren of the ambulance blared a few streets away.

'What's your name?' the mother called.

Jack didn't answer. He was thinking about his daughter, Lily. That's when he almost collided with a blue Escort. He thought about going after the car, but he was to blame, he'd stepped out without looking.

When Jack got home he threw off his wet clothes and jumped straight in the shower. He wasn't in bad shape for a forty-two-year-old who never exercised or watched his diet. He believed he had enough exercise doing his job, like the incident with the young boy in the park. He'd been chasing criminals for twenty years now and still loved the job. As he rubbed shampoo into his grey streaked, thick black hair, he thought about his wife and daughter.

Susan had decided she'd had enough of being a policeman's wife and had gone off with her boss at the estate agents to sell property in Spain. He remembered the day she told him and the row they had after dinner.

'I'm tired of you, Jack. I'm tired of your job, your drinking, your excuses for never being here.'

'I'm trying to support my family!' Jack insisted. 'Do you really think I want to go without sleep? Or miss my daughter's parents evening? I work hard for this family. I can't help that my job sometimes takes me away from it.'

'You're never here, Jack. Even when you are, you have your face in case files. I make arrangements for us to have dinner with friends and you never show up. Your mind's like a ball of fluff, blowing all over the place and settling nowhere. I can't take anymore! I'm leaving you!! I'm going to Spain with Jeff!'

He'd slapped her face then. The first time in his life he'd hit a woman. It wasn't so much her going with another man, it was the kick to his pride that hurt most. For months he'd suspected something between her and Jeff, the late hours, the unexplained meetings, but he hadn't wanted to admit it to himself. It would be like admitting he was a failure. He just tried to hold it together for Lily's sake. He grew up without a father, he didn't want that to happen to his daughter. In the end he had to accept there was nothing to hold them together anymore, not even Lily.

Susan stood at the foot of the stairs, her hand brushed the bright red mark on her cheek as she tucked loose strands of brown hair behind her ear.

'I'm not taking Lily. It won't do her any good to live in a strange country and I won't have time for her while we set up a new business. Perhaps she can come over in a couple of years.'

'Over my dead body! You go, you'll never take her!' said Jack.

'It's never really been about us, has it Jack?'

'What are you talking about?'

'Well, you're here, but you're not here. You're off in daydreams. You never really wanted this marriage in the first place. You wanted her, didn't you?'

'I don't know what you're talking about.' Jack looked away from her angry glare.

'Oh, I think you do! But she didn't want you, did she? She opted for the reliable doctor.'

Jack sighed. 'I don't want to hear this. Just go.'

She packed her bags and left.

Nine years had passed since that night. Jack and Lily had made a happy life together. He sold the family home and bought two flats above the gents' tailors in Dudstone. They lived in the one fronted the High Street. It was thirty yards from the police station where he worked, so he sometimes left his car on the station car park and walked home. There was a car park to the rear of the flat which he could use, but he had to unlock the huge gates and lock them again, then walk back round the block to the entrance to the flats.

The flat at the rear of the building he rented out to retired school mistress, Miss Stella Baker, who was in her seventies, and spent most of her time cross-stitching and listening to classical music. Jack had two of her stitched cottages on his lounge walls.

She'd given him one the last two Christmases, since Lily had gone. They'd spent many happy hours talking, or eating one of her delicious beef stews and Jack had grown very fond of her. She was a lady who couldn't face the day without her make-up. She dyed her long hair black and tied it back in a ponytail. Her make-up was a little too dark and made her look tanned. With red lipstick and a black pencil beauty spot just above her top lip, she reminded Jack of a gypsy who had come to his house selling clothes pegs. If she had to take any pills she would wrap them in a small piece of bread and swallow them with water. When Jack asked why she did this, she replied.

'Pills erode your stomach. Don't take them unless it's to save your life, Jack.' She'd taught French, mathematics and dance at a local school and lived in Dudstone all her life.

Lily had spent a lot of time with her during the long school holidays and had become fluent in French. Jack thought her relationship with Miss Baker had helped her to cope with her mother's absence.

That lovely girl had been his life. He was so proud of her and her ambition to be a primary school teacher, a career which had been influenced by her close relationship with Miss Baker. Now he'd lost her. He sometimes wished he'd let her go with her mother.

He was at work at the time she was taken, a little over two years ago. That was the only time Susan had been in touch with him. She phoned to ask what had happened to Lily, but never visited or showed any other interest in the disappearance of her only child.

Jack got out the shower, slipped on a bathrobe, grabbed a couple of sausage rolls from the fridge and went to sit in the lounge. On the wall facing him was a framed collection of sailors' knots that one of the fishermen had given him when he left Riley Cross. He worked on the boats with them long enough to learn how to do them all and had passed on his skill to Lily, which she practiced on him from an early age. He recalled the delight on her little face when he feigned being unable to get free from the ropes she tied round him.

His eyes filled with tears. He looked at the bottle of whiskey on the coffee table in front of him, as if it held the answers to all the questions in his shattered mind. Then he looked across the room at the picture of Lily displayed on the wall above a dining table which was cluttered with case files and the dust covered wooden boat kit he was in the process of making.

She was sixteen when it was taken. Her long blond hair was lifted up and styled into a bun on top of her head for the school prom. She looked just like his mother, Rose. Tears stung his eyes again and he wiped them away with the back of his hand.

He picked up the bottle of whiskey and opened it.

Sometimes he found it hard to go on. Many times he thought about killing himself. The only thing that stopped him was not knowing what had happened to Lily. He had to find her.

There'd been five females in Jack's life since Susan had gone. Mary, the hairdresser, who had quickly tired of Lily's clinging ways, Sally Dickson, a young DC, who got a promotion and moved down south, Miss Baker, his mother, and Lily. But Lily had gone and his mother blamed him. He made her a latchkey kid and although his mother never said it, he knew she thought he should have given up his job to be at home with his child. He sometimes wished he had but he couldn't leave now, he vowed he would find out what had happened to his girl, no matter how long it took.

He poured a glass of whiskey and looked at it. He got up and went to the kitchen and opened a wall cupboard. Two bottles of Johnny Walker and a bag of crushed pills. Waiting. Ready for bad news day. He checked the cupboard regularly, as if someone was going to sneak in and find his way out of dealing with the bad news that could come any day. He closed the cupboard, went back in the lounge, picked up his phone and scrolled to his mother's number. He hadn't called her this week.

A sleepy voice mumbled. 'Hello, who's that?'

'It's me, mother. I thought I'd give you a call to see how you are,' said Jack.

'You been drinking again?'

'No, I haven't.'

'Yet,' said his mother. 'Don't lie to me Jack.'

'Why do you always think I've been drinking when I call you? Can't we just have a proper conversation for once? Like normal people do.'

'I was asleep and you woke me up. Call me tomorrow,' said the old woman. Then added. 'When you're sober,' and hung up.

Jack sighed, picked up the glass of whiskey and swallowed it in one gulp. His mother was a force to be reckoned with.

When he moved to the West Midlands over eighteen years ago he found it hard to understand the dialect and accent. He remembered the first time he met Ted Bateman. They were both new on the force, but Ted had the advantage of being born and bred in the area. Jack was partnered with him while he got accustomed to the place and they'd been partners ever since. Ted introduced him to the Black Country dishes of bacon and grey peas, or 'bercon an grey pays', as the locals pronounced it, and faggots with mushy peas. Jack thought they looked like slop, but when he tasted them, he was hooked. He'd tried to cut down on them lately though after a recent blood test found he had a cholesterol reading of six point eight. 'Pack in the fags and have a low fat diet. No fish and chips or meat pies,' his doctor had told him after he refused to take statins. But he found it hard to do either.

It had taken quite a while to settle in Dudstone and Susan had complained constantly about having no friends and being stuck at home with a toddler. Money was tight and they lived in a rented flat for five years while they saved a deposit for a house. By the time Lily was in her third year at school they had their house and Susan seemed happy working part-time for a local estate agent. Little did he know that it was the beginning of the end for their marriage.

Chapter Six

It had been a close call. For a few minutes he thought he'd been seen and the sirens were the police coming after him. When the ambulance passed him at the end of the road he calmed down. He'd done it!

He watched her now. She lay motionless on the bed, as he took her clothes off to dress her in a soft white robe. He ran his hand along the contour of her thigh, up across her stomach and caressed her firm young breasts.

The bad voice told him, 'Go on. Take her. She is yours.'

'Get thee behind me Satan,' he whispered, as he covered her with the white robe and left the room. He slid the three bolts shut and went to write in his book. 'She must be perfect and obedient, like my angel Rebecca who was taken from me'. He rested the pen on the book and opened the brown cardboard box in front of him. The last ugly shoe. It was a kind of trophy for him now. That shoe had given him so much misery. It had dominated his early years like a terminal illness. Now he was master over it. He kept it in the box to remind him of the pain and heartache that had been inflicted upon him because of it. That shoe had become his motivation to set things right, to inflict on others what they had done to him.

An eye for an eye,' he murmured as he closed the lid.

His father's voice boomed in his head. 'Have you read the lesson for today, boy? The only path is the way of the righteous. We must all strive for perfection in what we do. The Lord has shown us the way. But with you, he sadly fails. Why are you so disobedient? Why do you make me so angry?'

The boy was nine years old, hiding behind the curtains in his bedroom, he shook like a leaf as he stood in a pool of urine.

His father stood in the doorway, an angry giant with the instrument of obedience in his hand. 'Get out from there! Lie across the bed and take your punishment like a man. You are a useless cripple! You have failed in your tasks again. What are you?'

'I am a useless cripple. I have failed to please my father,' the boy sobbed as he limped to the bed and laid belly down.

'And what do we do with useless, disobedient cripples?'

'We p… punish them, father.'

'It is written. We must not spare the rod. It is our salvation. As master of the house, I must put my household in order.' His father pulled down his pants and pushed the thing inside him. After a couple of minutes he withdrew the instrument and sodomised him. The boy bit his bottom lip to stop himself from crying out and tasted blood. All he could think of was the day when he would be free of the torture that was his life.

He shook himself from the dark memories of the past where that boy existed and switched on his laptop. The chat room was busy tonight. Lots of conversations about a new Xbox game and One Direction. He chatted with Molly Dancer and Sara-be-Good. They were two of his favourite friends. But his special girl wasn't on tonight and the signal kept going on and off. The dongle didn't work too well here. He would go on later when he was back at his house. He would have to leave the girls alone tonight, he had work to do tomorrow.

He checked his messages and emails and was about to sign out when her name popped up in the chat room. Goldilocks was online. He greeted her and told her he had been chosen to play for the school football team.

Catherine woke up. Her head throbbed, she felt weak and her lips were blistered and sore. She lay on a bed in a strange room. The white curtains were closed and a dim lightbulb cast shadows across the room. Where was this place? How did she get here? She was supposed to be going out with her friends after work. What had happened to her? Perhaps she'd had an accident. When she tried to sit up she found her hands and feet were tied to the bed posts with plastic twine. Her stomach rolled over and she started to shake. There was a man and a blue car. She'd been distracted by a commotion in the park. Was this a dream? Or had she really been kidnapped?

She looked round the room. Below the white curtains was a small sink, a cupboard beneath it and a toilet to the right of it. A mop and broom were propped up against the wall. The walls and ceiling were white, so was the door. It looked sterile, like a hospital ward.

Three bolts slid across on the other side of the door and it slowly opened. A figure dressed in a white gown walked in. A surgical mask covered the mouth and nose, and a white cap covered the hair.

'I thought you might be hungry.' He carried a tray. 'Hope you like eggs?' He spoke softly with the voice of a young man, as he limped across the room towards the bed.

Catherine looked from the tray to his face. Her vision blurred. 'Have I had an accident? 'Why am I here? Who are you?'

'Too many questions. I'm not going to hurt you.'

'I'd like to know why I'm here,' said Catherine.

'I told you, I'm not going to hurt you. I'm a doctor. You must call me "Doctor". You are here Catherine because you took the wrong path, because you didn't listen to the news and because you believed nothing like this would ever happen to you. Simply put, you are here because of your habits. You are a prime victim for kidnap or murder. But I've saved you from that. You are safe here.'

'You've been watching me? You've kidnapped me because of my habits? This is insane! I want to go home!'

'Don't shout. I don't like women who shout. I

might have to do something about it if you don't do as you're told.'

'Do what?' Catherine asked, with a shake in her voice.

He was tall and thin, almost skeletal. 'I might decide to cut out your tongue or operate on your vocal cords,' he said calmly, as if he was telling her the sun was shining. He put the tray on the bed. 'I've done it before and I must say it worked wonders on the bitch. I don't want to do it to you, so you must behave and respect me and do everything I say. The Lord tells us that women are the servants of men and I expect that from you. Now I'm going to untie your hands for you to eat this. If you try anything I will punish you.'

He took a scalpel from the tray and held it menacingly close to her face. 'This is the tool of my trade. I can make you beautiful or I can destroy your face and no man will ever look at you again, except in disgust. I don't want to use it but I will if you disobey me. Do you understand?'

Catherine swallowed hard and nodded. She wanted to scream but thought that might antagonise him. His blue eyes were a well of evil as he pressed the blade on her cheek. She took a deep breath, closed her eyes and waited for the cut. Her head throbbed and the twine cut into her wrists and ankles. She thought she would pass out.

The doctor scanned her face, a frown appeared round his eyes. 'Damn! You have a raised nevus above your right eye. I shall have to do something about that nasty bunch of melanocytes.' He went out of the room and came back a few seconds later.

Catherine opened her eyes. He stood by the bed with a syringe in his hand.

'No! Please!' She screamed. 'Please don't hurt me! I will do whatever you say.'

He carried her down the cellar steps to where his father used to do his experiments and research. The cellar stretched the entire length of the house and was divided into three sections. Section one was where his father kept his wines and spirits. There were still a few choice bottles, covered in cobwebs, and of no interest to him. A metal door led to section two, which was the laboratory and operating theatre. Another metal door led to section three which housed a generator. This was powered by a huge log or coal burning furnace, a throwback to the nineteen-twenties and a backup power supply when the electricity failed. He didn't use it because it made too much noise. He'd bypassed the electric meter and reconnected the power himself. In the third room there was also a couple of rusty industrial washing machines and a tumble dryer that the housekeeper, Mrs Cole, used, until she vanished off the face of the earth one winter's day in nineteen-ninety-six. His mother had complained bitterly about the old woman for going off and leaving her to do the 'damn washing'. His father had dropped her off at her house the night before, as he usually did. The police had come and asked the usual questions. No-one had a clue what had happened to her, and the old bag, who twisted his ear whenever they were alone, was never seen again.

New machines were installed upstairs in the kitchen because his mother hated doing the laundry in the cellar. He would have thrown these old machines out if he was going to live here permanently. He'd got no intention of ever doing that. This was a bad place.

He remembered the times he followed his mother and father down to the operating room. He'd heard them coming down here many nights and had used a screwdriver to make a hole in the wall behind the wine racks, so that he could watch them. His mother would lie on the table while his father turned on his classical music, usually Beethoven or Bach, put on his white gown, and then injected her with ketamine. This made her drowsy and pliable so that he could do whatever he wanted. Sometimes they had sex like dogs, sometimes he pushed objects inside her or sometimes he just slapped her about or whipped her backside until it glowed red.

When it was over his father would lean over and say something like, 'Shall I make you more beautiful, princess? What shall it be today?'

'I'll have the creases removed from round my eyes, master,' his semi-comatose mother would answer. Or, 'Make my lips like Marilyn Monroe's.'

The last one had almost made him laugh out loud.

His mother would appear the next day, her face swathed in bandages, with trout lips, her honey blond hair swept back and tied in a ponytail, slowly becoming a woman he didn't recognise. Not that she was anything like he imagined a mother to be. She was cold and aloof towards him. Not a drop of maternal instinct flowed through her veins, that space was taken up with gin and Jack Daniel's.

He thought about the other girls too, the ones that went down the cellar and never came back up. The ones his mother didn't know about.

Chapter Seven

Jack woke up cold. It was thirty minutes after midnight and he was hungry again. As he stood to go to the kitchen the phone rang. He picked it up and mumbled a gruff. 'Hello.'

'Sir, it's Constable Hadley. Sorry to disturb you but I need your advice on a matter that's just come in.'

'Don't I get time off, Hadley? Which one are you?'

Two new police constables and two police community support officers had recently joined the force and Jack had trouble remembering their names, even more so when he'd had a couple of whiskies.

'I'm the one they call Lofty, sir.'

'Okay. Tall, with blond hair?'

'Yes, sir.'

'What's up, Hadley?'

'A Mr and Mrs Bennett are here, sir. They're worried about their daughter, Catherine, who didn't come home from work or meet her friends as planned. What should I do, sir? They're convinced something has happened to her.'

'When and where did she go missing? And how old is she?'

'She left work at five-thirty, should have been home for six. She always walks the same route. None of her friends have seen her. The parents have called the girls she was supposed to meet. She's seventeen, sir. She works at the library at the end of Broad Street. She's been missing nearly seven hours now.'

'I was on Broad Street tonight. I stopped on my way home for… oh never mind what for. I didn't see anything suspicious, but I was preoccupied with something else.' Jack thought of the time when Lily had gone missing and all the hours that had been wasted by him and others, doing nothing but wait for her to show up because they wrongly assumed that she was with her friends. Almost half a day had been lost.

'I'm coming in, Hadley. Call DS. Bateman, DS Jones, Sergeant Poole and whoever else you can wake up. And I don't care what shift they were on. I want them at the station. If I can't get time off to sleep neither can they. Technically, because she's under eighteen she's a missing child.'

'Yes, sir.'

Jack grabbed a pair of crumpled jeans and a shirt from the wash basket, put them on, then shoved his feet into scuffed brown hush puppies. Within five minutes of hanging up the phone he was at the station.

The girl, Catherine, had gone missing in daylight hours, she was the same age as Lily when she went missing and she'd been taken within a quarter of a mile of the college where Lily had gone missing.

Jack's mind went into overdrive. It was the same kidnapper, it had to be. He didn't want to think about the word 'killer'. Would he finally find out what had happened to his precious daughter? For two years he'd tried to link every missing girl to Lily's case, but this might be too close to be a coincidence.

*

When Catherine woke up her head was bandaged and she could feel a dull pain above her right eye. The doctor hovered in front of her.

'I had to take that unsightly thing off your face. That's something I didn't notice during our brief interview. I might decide to do other improvements when I've examined you thoroughly. If there's one thing I don't like it's an ugly, nagging woman, so I don't want to hear any complaints. When you're feeling better we will celebrate our union. You know, Catherine, I have waited so long for you to come in to my life. Everything is ready for the ceremony. You only have to pass one test, and I'm sure you will do it. But the time isn't right yet. We have to wait for that to heal before we seal our marriage.'

'What interview? I can't remember.' A tear rolled down her face. She tried to move and found a drip attached to her hand. She trembled.

'Well that's something for you to think about, Catherine. It will occupy your mind for a while. I'm not going to give you any clues. That drip is to give you medication. We don't want you catching an infection, do we? I think you might be a little overweight, so I'll give you less food until you reach ideal weight. You have to fit into the dress I've bought. It's a size eight.' He talked away, as if they had conversations like this every day.

Catherine stared at the ice blue eyes. Had she heard that voice before? She wasn't sure. Her thoughts were all jumbled. She wasn't fat, she was a size twelve. Was this man going to starve her to death? She couldn't think clearly. Perhaps she was in hospital. What had happened to her? Who was he who hovered around her and the voice that came out of nowhere and echoed in her mind?

'Not very talkative are we, Catherine? That's the medication working. I suppose it's a bit of a shock to wake up and find you have a new life. Never mind, you'll soon get used to it. Just as you will get used to your new name 'Rebecca' when we are married. All you have to do is be obedient and I will treat you like a princess. You will have tasks to do each day when you're feeling better. Homes can only run smoothly when everyone knows their place and the quicker you learn yours, the easier your life will be. You will be the crown of my life.' He pulled a syringe from the pocket of his white coat. 'Just a little something to make you sleep.'

Catherine screamed as he stuck it in her arm. She tried hard to keep her eyes open, but they were so heavy and a comfortable feeling flowed through her veins.

In another room the other girl woke up with a start. She thought she heard someone scream. It was quiet now. A few hours earlier the sound of doors opening and closing had sent her mind in turmoil. What had the doctor been doing? She felt as if she was living on the edge of a precipice and the ground she sat on was slowly eroded beneath her. Any minute she could slip into the darkness, the abyss he'd built around her, to control and torture her into submission. She had learned how to answer him, how to look at him and how not to look at him. These were things he could see and hear. But he couldn't see the thoughts in her mind or the hatred for him that festered in her heart.

When she stole the pen from the lounge he didn't feed her for five days. He tortured her first and then left her with only water from the tap in her room to drink.

The pain had been unbearable as he pushed a nail file down the inside of her fingernails and ripped them off. Three of her nails were missing when she passed out and her fingers were septic for weeks. They'd grown back now, but every time she looked at them she winced. The doctor wanted a perfect woman, yet the punishment he netted out left her scarred and full of hatred. Stealing that pen had sealed her fate and everything had gone downhill since then.

It was during those days when he left her to starve that she began to count time. The tap dripped and when she turned it off fully, it still dripped. She thought each drip was about a second apart. She stood at the sink and counted every drip until her plastic beaker was full. It took about twelve hundred drips to fill the beaker. Every full beaker was twenty minutes. She filled up the plastic bowl she washed in and kept filling up the beaker. The bowl held thirty beakers of water, so it took about ten hours to fill. She knew it wasn't accurate but it helped to stop her thinking of all the bad things the doctor had done to her, of the pain in her fingers, and it gave her a rough idea how many days she'd been here. So far she'd counted seven hundred and forty but it could have been a lot more.

She had no idea how long she'd been here before she stole the pen. A few times she'd woken up and the bowl had been overflowing, so she had to guess the hours. Once the Doctor had emptied the bowl and she had to guess how much water had been in there. It upset her when this happened. She had a routine, which in a way helped to give some normality to her abnormal existence. She knew if the bowl was nearly full she'd slept more than eight hours. She scratched marks on it with a hair clip, which was the only thing the doctor hadn't taken from her, because he hadn't seen it in her hair. Quarter full, half full, three-quarters full, the bowl was her clock, the most important thing in her miserable life, and even if her timing was way off the mark, she felt compelled to stick to it, to make her feel she had a reason to go on, as her life's seconds dripped down the sink.

She thought of simple things she'd taken for granted, like an ice cream, a jam doughnut, or a walk in the park. She regretted not telling her father she loved him, and arguing with him on the day she was taken because she wanted to stay over at her friend's and he said 'no'. She missed her nana too.

The hair clip was her only tool, a secret that the Doctor didn't know about, but it was no good to try and open locks. There was no lock on the door or keyhole. He shut her in with three bolts on the other side of the door. She counted them sliding across as he came and went. She was good at counting. There were eighteen tiles along the top of the small work surface, three had cracks in them, two were off-white.

Count, count, count. That's all she did.

The Doctor would come daily to examine her. He'd poke his fingers inside her and sometimes he touched himself. That was bad enough but not half as painful or disgusting as the other thing he pushed into her. She didn't know what it was at first, all she knew was that it was the worst pain she'd ever endured. The object was long and hard and he told her not to look, but she did once and he went crazy. He beat her, kicked her and threatened to take her eyes out.

Now she always kept her eyes tightly closed. She'd learned the hard way that he didn't make idle threats. The torture tool was an old club-shaped wooden police truncheon with a rippled handle and leather strap. He called it the 'tool of obedience'.

He hadn't raped her with it for a long time. Perhaps because she was pregnant and he didn't want to harm his baby. The baby kicked all the time now and no matter how hard she tried to hate it, she couldn't. It was a prisoner, a victim just like herself, it was the only contact she had with anything like another person. The Doctor wasn't a person, he was a vile monster. She'd never seen his face, he always wore a surgical mask, but she would never forget those evil blue eyes.

*

Michael sat in the lounge. He'd been reading from the Bible and something he read about suffering had jogged his memory of the time he'd been locked away.

Doctors and psychiatrists were brought from all

over the country to examine him and probe his mind to determine if he was a 'normal' child. They were all fooled by his little-boy-lost look, his innocence, his love of animals. They listened intently as he told them what had happened the night his parents died.

'My father was drunk and he and my mother were shouting downstairs. When I went down he said he was going to kill all of us. I tried to run out of the house but I tripped and hit my head on the table in the hall. I don't know what happened after that.' Then he cried. It was an Oscar winning performance.

They kept him in the carbolic and bleach-smelling home for disturbed children for a year, every day instilling the rules of the institution. Rule one. I must clean my room and make my bed. Rule two. I must be respectful to those above me. There was a list as long as his arm. He never disobeyed any. He knew they wouldn't keep him there until he was eighteen, they couldn't justify locking up such a sweet, respectful child, he must be given the chance of a normal upbringing. But what was normal? The staff there carried on where his father had left off, with their strict rules and punishment.

He would take it though, he was used to much worse than they could ever imagine.

He behaved like a saint.

He was moved to the children's home when he was eleven, to wait and hope to be adopted by loving parents but no-one ever came. He was left there with the other cripples and half-castes that nobody wanted, to rot and fester and plan his revenge.

He used his captivity to study. The home had three

computers the children could take turns to use. He was online every opportunity he had and began to look at clinics throughout Europe where he could get treatment to lengthen his left leg.

He hated the home and the people in it. But the people he hated more were the ones who had put him there. The young social worker Miss Grey, and the chairman of the committee, Henry Chapman, who decided he should be locked away to be tested, probed and abused by people who treated him as cruelly as his father had. They would pay for what had happened to him. They still lived close by, had their lovely happy lives, totally unaware that he was watching them.

Catherine coughed and he was worried she might get an infection, like the first girl. That girl had too many imperfections on her body. He'd cut several warts off her back and arms, some of them had scarred, some had become infected. It was her own fault he cut her vocal cords. That operation hadn't gone well at all and she couldn't swallow anything after. But she argued so much and he could no longer control her with threats of violence. She laughed at him and used the gutter language from where she came. She certainly wasn't the kind of wife who would be obedient and honour him as her master, or be his crown. She was a slut. She'd gone downhill fast after she stopped eating and drinking. When he hit her with the hammer, it was an act of mercy. He thought she would die quickly. It took five days.

Now she was in the garden shed and the smell was unbearable. He would have to get rid of her. He wasn't worried about anyone finding her. No-one ever came here and the shed was too far round the back of the house for anyone to notice the stench.

She had to go because there could be another one in there any day.

Chapter Eight

'Hadley, get me the report on the Bennett girl,' said Jack, as he passed the polished oak front desk of the hundred-year-old police station to get to his office.

'And could you put some coffee on, lad?' He opened his office door and the night's heat rushed out. 'Where are the parents?'

'In room one, sir. They insisted on staying until you got here. DS. Bateman's with them.'

'Good. Well, get the kettle on, lad, we're probably in for a long night.'

DS Mickey Jones emerged from a side office, his hair slicked back with enough grease to cook a bowl of chips. He looked at Jack.

'Girl goes missing and all hell breaks loose. A few days off eighteen. She's probably in the park getting laid.'

'She's not that kind of girl!' Hadley snapped.

'Get the coffee on, Hadley,' said Jack. He waited for Hadley to disappear down the corridor then spoke to Jones. 'That's not the attitude I expect from one of my senior officers. One of these days that mouth of yours will get you in a lot of trouble.'

'We all have to get out of bed because you're having a panic attack,' said Jones.

'Shut it, Jones! She's a child gone missing. I don't care what she's been doing. I sincerely hope she is in the park with a lad and not in some maniac's grasp.'

'You're obsessed,' Jones mumbled as he walked off down the corridor towards the kitchen.

'What was that?' Jack shouted after him.

'I said "yes sir",' Jones called back over his shoulder.

Jack shook his head. Mickey Jones had the ability to always rub him up the wrong way. 'Sarcastic bastard,' he muttered under his breath.

Within five minutes Hadley came with two steaming cups and a packet of digestives on a flowery tray. 'The computers are down again, sir. I've called the technician in to have a look at them. I think they're a bit outdated sir. We need new ones.'

Jack glanced at the two cups. 'Well nothing works right in this place, Hadley. I think you'll get a positive 'no' from the superintendent for that suggestion. Did the plumber come to fix the leak in the gents? I nearly did the splits in there this morning.'

'Yes, sir.' Hadley grinned and showed a set of perfectly white teeth.

'What's so funny?'

'The thought of you doing the splits, sir.'

'Yes. Well sit down and tell me what you know about Catherine Bennett.'

'I know Catherine very well and I don't think she would go off anywhere without telling someone.' He put a hand through his short blond hair and sat down.

Jack jumped out of his seat. 'You know her? Why didn't you tell me this on the phone?'

'You sounded a bit p… angry that I'd called, sir.' Hadley cringed slightly. 'But you did tell me to call you if we had any reports of missing girls, and I've got something else to tell you.'

'Well? What?' Jack took a biscuit from the tray and dunked it in his coffee.

'I took the liberty of phoning some people who are mutual friends, sir. I felt I had to do something. She's such a lovely girl.'

'And?'

'They all think the same as me, sir. She's been taken. No-one's seen or heard from her. Here's the list of people I've called.'

'Ten points for initiative, Hadley. I'm going in to see her parents.' Jack stopped at the door. 'Did you let the two drunks out?'

'Yes, sir. Joey Coombs said, "I'm going to sue that effing Riley for wrongful arrest." And Smithy said, "He's insulted me as well". I think he meant assaulted, sir, he showed me a bruise on his knee.'

Jack laughed. 'Well Joey always says that, and Smithy fell over my foot, the cheeky bugger. They're a couple of rogues, Hadley, but usually nothing more serious than receiving stolen goods or petty theft.'

Catherine's father, a tall, dark haired man in his mid-forties stood and introduced himself. 'I'm the Reverend John Bennett and this is my wife, Hannah. I'm the minister for Saint Edmunds. We live at The Rectory on the far end of Broad Street.'

John Bennett had beads of sweat on his brow, which he dabbed intermittently with a white handkerchief. His wife sat in a chair, head bowed, quietly crying. Ted Bateman sat opposite them with a note pad, a pen and a picture of Catherine on the table in front of him.

Jack picked up the picture and looked at it. 'I'm sorry we have to ask these questions, Mrs Bennett, but we need to know as much about Catherine as we can.

Some of my colleagues are getting ready to interview the staff at the library. We need to get a complete account of what she did and where she went yesterday. Other officers will be making house to house enquiries along the route Catherine takes to and from work. Also I want to know if she had a boyfriend she might have met after work, and names and addresses of all her friends. Has she taken her passport, credit cards or any clothes with her? Has she been upset about anything? What was she wearing? Clothes? Jewellery? Does she have any birthmarks or scars?'

'Catherine does not have boyfriends,' said Mr Bennett sternly. 'We don't encourage it. The young men of today don't want commitment or marriage, they just want a good time. Irresponsible most of them.'

'She's taken nothing with her, Inspector Riley,' Mrs Bennett looked up. She was a good looking woman, with fair hair and blue eyes, like her missing daughter. 'I would have known. Catherine is a very open girl. She has no secrets from us. She always tells us where she's going, who with and what time she'll be back. This is why we're so worried. We just know she wouldn't do anything like this. Someone must have taken her.' She put her hands to her face and sobbed.

This was part of the job Jack didn't like. He'd been here before, it should have been second nature, but he had that uncomfortable feeling in his chest, he could understand exactly how they felt at this moment.

'We've said all this to Andrew, Inspector,' said John Bennett.

'Andrew?'

'Constable Hadley. He and Catherine know each other through mutual friends.'

'Yes. Well it never hurts to go through it again. There could be something else you'd like to add, or something we've overlooked.'

'She has a small brown mole above her right eyebrow, Inspector,' said John Bennett. 'As my wife said, we've checked her room. As far as we can see nothing is missing. She is a very happy girl, there are no problems at home. She has always been obedient.'

Bateman took notes.

'I'd like to add it would be better to get on with looking for our daughter, Inspector.' Hannah Bennett had stopped crying and looked at Jack accusingly.

'We've wasted precious hours all ready.' She stood up and moved to the door.

'We'll do everything we can to find Catherine, Mrs Bennett. Now I think you'd be better off at home in case she turns up. And try to get some rest.'

'We will pray for her safe return,' said John Bennett as he wiped his brow and followed his wife out.

Jack sat in his office thinking about the pain he saw in Hannah Bennett's eyes.

When Lily went missing everyone involved in the case, including himself, had thought she would turn up at a friend's house. Hannah Bennett knew her daughter was missing because something bad had happened to her and he didn't think her father's prayers would make any difference to the outcome.

He'd prayed during the early days of Lily's absence. Then the days turned to weeks, then months, then years. After a while all hope faded, the prayers ceased and he felt nothing but resentment that his girl had gone. Any good parent would do anything to protect their young, even talk to an invisible being they didn't believe existed.

Obsessed with his efforts to find her he'd accused people of lying and covering up, then finally had a breakdown and was off work for a year. He hoped he wouldn't crack again. It had taken months for the obsession to abate. He still had the same determination to find Lily, but he knew that if he didn't control it, he would get nowhere. He had to get back on the job so that he would be there if anything turned up. Catherine Bennett had been taken in similar circumstances and there was a strong possibility the kidnapper was the same person who had taken Lily.

Chapter Nine

Doctor Steve Munroe finished his work shift at Bordley General Hospital at 2am. He was exhausted when he got home and went straight to bed. After barely two hours sleep he woke up in a sweat. The nightmares he suffered as a teenager were back.

It was always the same dream. He was being pulled into a fire. As the flames began to engulf him he woke up. He laid awake for hours after the dream, trying to find the face of the person in his mind.

Lack of sleep was beginning to affect his concentration during the day. Strange images flashed into his mind whenever he sat to rest for a moment, or to fill in his case notes. Long dark corridors appeared from nowhere, someone screamed, a door slammed, a fire raged, a woman with the face of a plastic doll, laughed at him, while her face melted and fell away like something from a horror movie. If he carried on like this his job at the hospital would be at risk. He thought he was going out of his mind and wondered what had happened in the past that could have caused these waking images.

His real parents had died and he couldn't remember anything about them after an accident at the children's home left him with amnesia. He was convinced the nightmares and day-mares had something to do with his real family. His adoptive parents had never mentioned his past and he was apprehensive about bringing the subject up, but he felt the answer to the strange dreams lay in finding out who he really was and where he came from.

He'd been happy with his adoptive parents since he'd gone to live with them at the age of twelve. He wanted to be a doctor and they financed his studies through medical school, bought him his first car when he graduated and encouraged him to realise his ambitions. Lately, strange thoughts about them had disturbed him. Were they really who they said they were? What was before them? Why was he even thinking like this? Faces of strangers floated around him like ghosts. He tried to place them, but they turned to smoke and vanished into thin air. He had to find out about his family, then perhaps the nightmares and bad thoughts would end.

Chapter Ten

The girl had her ear to the door. The Doctor had gone out. He used to let her out once a day to walk round the house and have a warm bath. Lately he'd missed days. She was glad but at the same time suspicious of what he might be doing instead of coming to her. The last few weeks he'd spent more time away, which meant she was left without food for longer. When he did come to her, he poked and prodded her stomach and gave her internal examinations, he said, to check that the baby was okay, but she knew he gained some kind of perverted sexual pleasure because he usually raped her when the examination was over. In her mind she saw him as the evil incarnation of Doctor Frankenstein, from Mary Shelley's novel and Doctor Mengele, who performed cruel operations on thousands of men, women and children in German prison camps during the Second World War.

This room was her prison. The painted window blocked out day and night. Time ticked away in drips. Sometimes she sat for hours counting the seconds, wondering if it was light or dark beyond the window. She didn't like the dark and had always slept with a night light on. That was the only thing she didn't have to worry about here. The light stayed on all the time. The baby kicked. She put a hand on her stomach and began to sing 'Beautiful Dreamer'. This was the only time the Doctor didn't own her, the time she defied his rule not to make a noise. This was the song Daddy used to sing when she was young and it made her feel as if she existed in the other world, the comfort place, where she was safe. There was nothing good about this place, her other life was a million miles away. A cold sore on her lip itched and her ankles were swollen like balloons. The baby could come any time. What would she do with it? There was nothing here for a baby. She wished she could talk to her daddy's friend, Gwen, who had been so kind to her when her mother left. She told Gwen everything and moaned about her dad, and Gwen never once told on her. She would know what to do. So would Nana, who she missed so much. She smiled to herself. Nana and Daddy always argued about the slightest thing. She couldn't understand why they didn't get on with each other. Her stomach rumbled. She was so hungry and so tired.

A door slammed. The girl jumped up from her sleep. Was he in the room with her? She couldn't focus her eyes. 'Look at the door!' A voice screamed in her mind. She sat up slowly. He wasn't there. It must have been a dream. Beads of sweat dripped from her chin. How much longer could she take this? When would this torment end?

The Doctor had been out twice but he was back

now. She could hear him as he moved about the house. Perhaps he was going to starve her. Hunger had become her best friend as well as her obsession. She dreamt about food all the time, fish and chips, doughnuts and chocolate. Sometimes she thought death would be the only way out of this hell.

The tones of a funeral march started up and terror struck like a knife in her heart.

What was he going to do now? What perversion was he going to inflict upon her? The last time he'd tried to pop her eyeballs out of their sockets, while calmly telling her how it had been easy to do it to frogs. She still had pain around her eyes and nose. That torture was punishment for asking for more food.

Catherine opened her eyes. Had she heard someone singing, or was it a dream? Silence filled the room. She wondered what her parents were doing. Her mother was emotionally fragile. It was one of the reasons Catherine had always been careful to tell her mother where she was going. To stop her worrying. She'd seen her mother in one of her breakdowns when her Uncle George had fallen from a ladder as he cleaned their windows. He died right in front of her. Her mother carried the guilt for that like a lead weight hanging round her neck. Catherine tried so hard not to cause worry for her mother. This would make her ill again. She was used to keeping secrets that would make her mother ill. Secrets that no-one should know about. She couldn't possibly worry her mother with what her father had done.

She heard music. 'The Funeral March of the Marionette' by Charles Gounod. It was one her father had in his collection. It sent a chill through her. She heard the flap on the peephole drop and the three bolts slide across. The door opened. He limped into the room and sat on the bed to check her drip.

'I have some pills for you to take. They won't hurt you. They're vitamins to help prevent an infection.'

Catherine shook with fear. Was he going to poison her now? Was this her final moment? She was going to die. Tears ran down her face.

He leaned towards her and stroked her cheek. 'Don't cry, Rebecca. I'm not going to hurt you, I promise. Do you like my music? This particular one was the theme music for 'Alfred Hitchcock Presents'. Don't you think it's just right for a suspense thriller?' He closed the door and went to the lounge to see who was online in the chat room. His girl wasn't on so he switched off the laptop.

He'd dumped the body in a ditch on a nature reserve two miles from Dudstone.

That would give Inspector Riley something to think about. He hadn't tried to hide it. He wanted it to be found and had deliberately looked for a well-trodden path. He'd stripped her naked, hosed the body down with hot water and wrapped her in a black plastic sheet on the day she died. She'd been in the shed for over a week and the place was full of flies and maggots. He would clean it out tomorrow.

Touching the dead girl had excited him and he thought of Catherine and what he could do to her. He wanted to touch her, to feel her soft skin again, to pull and push and mould her to become his. He opened one of two books on the table and began to write.

I have to wait until the time is right. It has to be a special day. I will take Rebecca to my house and she will wear the clothes I have ready. We will be together for the rest of our lives, our children will be perfect and my Rebecca will be my crown, to love and care for me as she did before.

The other book was his father's, a prominent cosmetic surgeon, who had enjoyed world-wide fame he received from his writing. He didn't miss his parents. They were disappointed with him. This was why he changed his name. He didn't want the family name after the torture and misery his father had inflicted upon him. He could hear his father's voice bellowing along the dark corridors. 'He will never be a doctor! How have I produced something like this? What have I done to deserve this?'

He was determined to prove his father wrong. He didn't need to pass exams to be a better surgeon than his father. The house was full of all the books he needed. He would show them all. He put on his blond wig, surgical gown, hat and mask and went to feed the other girl before he left.

'Lie on the bed!' he shouted at the girl's door.

She heard the metal flap on the peephole drop. She laid down. The bolts slid across one, two, three and the door swung open. He carried a tray across the room and put it on the small table beside her bed. There were two slices of bread and some baked beans on the plate.

'Eat,' he said and went to go back out.

'Please, Doctor,' the girl called to him, 'may I have a baby book to read?' As soon as the words left her mouth his back straightened as if a puppeteer had pulled a string to make him stand up tall. She knew the encounter wouldn't end well.

The Doctor turned quickly, anger flashed in his eyes. His right eye began to twitch. 'Motherhood is a natural state for all women! You do not need books, you will know what to do. They didn't have books in Noah's day, they knew how to look after a baby, they squatted over birth bricks and gave birth in a hole in the ground. You have the luxury of a bed, you ungrateful bitch! Besides, you will only use it against me and try to make messages with the pages for others to see. Like the other one did.'

'Oh, no, Doctor, I wouldn't. I know how lucky I am to have you to look after me. I would never betray you.' She wondered how the other one was. She hadn't heard her for days and was beginning to think she had died or he'd moved her somewhere else. Her constant moaning had been heart-breaking. Was she the one who'd screamed?

The Doctor's eyes softened and his voice was calmer. 'I will think about it.' He hadn't forgiven her for taking the pen. She was spoiled now. She had lured him into committing sin, just like the bad Eve had. It was women like her who made men lust after the flesh. He unfastened his trousers. He wasn't sure what he would do with her once the baby was born. That was another matter to think about.

'Lie on your stomach, close your eyes and be still.' He pulled her robe up and took her pants off. 'Do not ask for anything. You must learn obedience and respect,' he said over and over as he raped her.

In the other room, Catherine tried to place the

song she thought she heard someone singing. She remembered watching an old black and white film about a giant ape with her mother. People tried to capture him and the heroine had sung 'Beautiful Dreamer' to make him calm. She suddenly felt sick. How long had it been since she'd eaten? She couldn't remember. Her head began to spin.

Suddenly he was in the room. Another needle in her arm.

'Good…night Re..bec..ca,' a voice from the void, which sounded like an old record player as it winded down.

A door closed.

Chapter Eleven

Saturday, 7am

The team assembled and waited for Jack's instructions. There were about two dozen of them in the room now, sat on desks and chairs. They drank coffee and talked in hushed tones. Pictures of Catherine were pinned to a board, along with a map of the area where she'd gone missing. There was also a timetable of her last known movements and a list of names of people she'd spoken to on Friday.

Jack stood in front of the board. He felt drained. All the emotions he had when Lily went missing were back. His legs were like jelly. He hoped his anxiety wouldn't make him breathless, vomit or pass out. DS Jones sat on the table in front of him with a grin on his face that irritated Jack no end. Ted sat next to Jones and picked at a small scab on his brow.

The room hushed as he spoke with a shake in his voice. 'Right, people. We have a missing girl, Catherine Bennett. She's seventeen and her parents insist she would never run away or go anywhere without telling them where she was going. She works at the library in town. Her mobile phone is switched off. She made a call at three-thirty to her friend, Alice Brown. We have no evidence yet, but I want you to proceed as you would with any missing person, bearing in mind it could be an abduction.

Speak to all the people on this list and check all the places Catherine has visited with her friends or on her own. This is the latest picture, taken about two years ago when she left school. I want a thorough search made along the route Catherine walks to and from work. Talk to the staff at the library to see if she mentioned a boyfriend, or any place she might have gone after work. I've checked with the phone company to see where the last signal was and it was on Broad Street around the time she went missing. I've also asked for a list of all phone activity during the last two weeks. It's possible she could have recently met someone at the library or one of the clubs she visited. A blue Escort was seen parked in Broad Street, which is where she lives with her parents. I was in the area and saw the car. I stepped out in front of it but had other things on my mind and didn't notice who was driving it. I have vague recollections that the driver wore some kind of cap, perhaps a baseball cap. It was only a fleeting glimpse. Look at CCTV footage along the route towards the town centre. Right, get your teams out. I'll leave you to delegate DS. Bateman. I'll be in my office if you need me.'

DS Jones leaned and whispered to Bateman, 'He didn't see anything because he was probably pissed up again.'

'Shut your dirty mouth,' said Bateman. 'And go

and do what you're supposed to be doing. You can check the CCTV images along Broad Street and at the library.'

Jones gave Bateman a sneering smile. 'He'll crack up again. Just remember who said it first.'

*

He watched them all file out of the meeting and turned to his colleague. 'I'm just going to grab a coffee. I won't be long.' He headed towards the canteen. He would sit near Bateman and Poole and listen in to what had been said in the meeting.

*

Someone tapped on Jack's door and Ted Bateman came in without waiting for an answer. 'Are you okay, Jack?' He picked at the scab on his brow.

Jack looked up. 'Yes, I'm fine, Ted.'

Ted looked at him for a long moment. 'I hope you don't mind me saying this, but you look like shit.' He inspected the debris in his fingernails.

'I feel like shit to be honest. I just can't help but notice the similarities with…'

Jack looked down at the file on his desk.

'Lily?' said Ted, before he could finish.

'I can't help it, Ted. This girl going missing has brought it all back and I feel raw.'

'I can understand that Jack. The same area around the college, another student. It's bound to affect you. I'd just like you to know I'm here for whatever you want me to do, whether it's in line with the job or not. I just want you to tell me if you start to feel you can't cope with it. You know I'll cover for you with anything, but you have to keep me in on it.'

Jack felt a lump rise in his throat. Ted had been with him all through the time of Lily's disappearance, right up to his breakdown and after. He was the one who had encouraged Jack back to work.

'Thanks Ted,' his voice was hoarse.

'Do you mind if I smoke?'

'Chuck one over here,' said Jack. 'I'm not doing too good at giving up. Have you seen the pictures of Catherine Bennett? She's the image of Lily.'

'Yes, that's exactly what I thought too. The teams are out looking for her. They're visiting the clubs she frequented with her friends. DCI Murray is on his way in.'

'Bloody hell! That's all we need!' Jack put Lily's file in a drawer. 'What did you make of the Bennetts, Ted?'

'Well, I thought he was a bit on edge. He was sweating like a pig. I know that could have been the stress of the situation.'

'I'm more concerned with the way he spoke. How many parents use the term "obedient" to describe their kids?'

'He's a preacher, Jack. The Bible is full of the word.'

'I suppose so. Perhaps I'm just looking for something that's not there.'

'He reminded me of that old actor in the vampire movies. What's his name? Christopher Lee.' Ted chuckled. 'When it comes to kids, Jack, you never know how they'll turn out. Take my brother's two lads. One's doing marine biology and the other's doing something with computers. Both at university. Now my two lads are totally different. One thinks he's the new Mick Jagger and plays in a rock band. The other calls himself an artist. He paints pictures of people with eyes up their arsehole and actually sells them! I mean, who in the world wants to hang things like that on their walls? Am I so far behind with the times?'

'Jack laughed. You're allowing them to make their own choices. Nothing wrong with that!'

'There's a distinct smell of smoke in here, Riley!' Murray opened the door to Jack's office and came in. He'd acquired a nose like a bloodhound since he'd given up smoking three years previously, after a heart attack that nearly killed him. He was down on everyone who still smoked.

Jack stood up and sniffed the air. 'Can't say I can smell anything, sir.'

'Well, you wouldn't, would you? You're the smoker. Anyway, fill me in on the missing girl. I'm speaking to the press later today.' He settled himself in a chair opposite Jack's and stroked his bushy, grey moustache. His cheeks looked like a baboon's arse and his bulbous purple nose betrayed years of heavy drinking. His hair, which he grew long at the sides, with partings just above each ear, was swirled and stuck to the top of his bald head like a giant Walnut Whip. He took a pill box from his coat pocket, opened it, shook some out on to his palm, threw them in to his mouth, then leaned across the desk and took Jack's cup of coffee to swallow them. 'Fucking pills! Give me acid, they do.'

Jack coughed. 'Well sir, her name's Catherine Bennett. She lives at The Rectory on the end of Broad Street. Her father's the vicar at Saint Edmunds. She was on her way home from work at the library when she went missing. We haven't got a lot to go on yet. We're looking at CCTV. There's also the sighting of the blue Escort, which I saw myself and believe could be linked to Lily's disappearance. If I remember right a blue car was seen in the vicinity when Lily was taken.'

Murray gave Jack a 'here we go again' look. 'This isn't about Lily, Jack, it's about Catherine Bennett, so don't get thinking too far ahead of yourself on this.'

'No, sir, I just thought…'

'You know what happened last time and I'd hate to have to do that again, Jack. You're a good copper. Stick to the case in hand until you can offer me a definite link. I suppose you've put all the usual procedures in operation?' He got up, burped loudly and opened the door.

'Yes, sir.' Jack ran a hand down the side of his face and across his mouth and felt the roughness of a two-day beard. 'House to house, friends and family being interviewed, checks on her mobile phone and CCTV at the library and along the route she took.'

'Good. Oh, and another thing,' Murray said as he went out. 'There's a DS. Sandy Morgan joining us from Yorkshire division. A profiler with a special interest in kidnappings, so I hear.' He leaned back in to the room before he closed the door.

'I'm drafting extra officers in from Segmore and

Tipley next Saturday. There's a demonstration organized to show opposition to the planned new mosque. It's supposed to be peaceful but you never know what will happen.'

'I'll be available if you need me, sir.'

'Thanks. I've had word a van load of electrical goods have been stolen in Dover and are on route to the West Midlands. Make everyone aware of it. I'll be getting a fax with a full list later today or tomorrow. How are the two new PCSOs getting on? Macdonald and Parker, isn't it?'

'Mackenzie and Parker, sir. DS. Bateman tells me they're good lads. I've only seen them two or three times since they've been here. They were called in to man the desk this morning. Everyone else is on the Bennett case.'

'Good. Mind Jones's promotion doesn't go to his head. I don't want him picking on them or the new PCs, Hadley and Wallace. We were lucky to get them transferred from Birhampton. We've been understaffed for two years now with all the cutbacks. I'm not keen on the idea of recruiting more volunteers.'

'Me neither, sir.'

'Try to tidy yourself up a bit, Jack. You're beginning to look like a down-and-out.'

He looked at Jack's bare ankles. 'And put some bloody socks on.' He burped again. 'Fucking acid! I'm sure there's a volcano in my gut!'

Jack smiled to himself as the door closed.

Chapter Twelve

Catherine woke up to find her hands and feet were no longer tied to the bed. The drip was gone and a large red bruise covered her hand just above the knuckles where it had been attached. She touched above her eye where the small brown mole had been. It felt sore and bumpy. The mad man had performed an operation on her.

She wondered what he would do next.

Slowly she eased herself to the edge of the bed and stood up. She was light-headed and her mouth felt like sandpaper as she walked unsteadily across the room.

She tried to reach over the sink to push the window open but it was shut tight. A wave of panic washed over her as she fell against the sink and gripped the edge to stop herself from falling over.

The Doctor had dressed her in a long fleecy white robe while she'd been unconscious. She shuddered at the thought of him touching her and seeing her naked.

In a small drawer under the sink she found ladies' pants, soap, toothbrush and paste and a towel. She had a wash and cleaned her teeth, then waited for him to come. If starving her was part of the plan to make her obedient it was working. She had no idea how long she'd been here, she was ravenous and would eat whatever he gave her, even if it was disgusting. She could close her mind to what he might do to her, she was good at switching off her emotions. She had to survive. If there was a way out she would find it, but as she scanned the room her hopes faded. The walls had no obvious signs of weaknesses, the window was firmly locked and the door was solid hardwood with no handle or keyhole.

Saturday, 11am

'Inspector, there's a Mrs White here to see you,' Ted Bateman stood in the doorway of Jack's office. He picked at the small scab on his brow.

'What about?'

'She was in the park yesterday. We found her when we were doing house to house. She said she saw a blue car in the vicinity of the park at the time Catherine Bennett went missing.'

'Okay, bring her in, Ted.'

'The mon from the off-licence told me yow were a policeman.' The heavily pregnant young woman waddled in and took a seat opposite Jack. 'I wanted to thank ya for saving me little boy's life.' She bent forward to retrieve something from her bag. 'I got ya this.' She pushed a bottle of Johnny Walker across the desk. 'I remember ya from the papers, two years ago, when ya daughter went missing. I'm so sorry about that. It must be terrible to go to bed at night wondering where she is.'

'Thank you. I don't think I can take your gift though. I was only doing my job.'

'Yow tek it. Goo on, hide it in the drawer. I'm not going to tell anyone, Inspector. I tek my Robbie to that park every day and I've noticed there's bin a blue Escort parked theer a few times lately. It was theer yesterday. Do ya remember?'

'I do. I was in a bit of a hurry to get home to change my clothes.' Jack gave her a quick smile as he picked the bottle up and put it in a drawer. 'Is Robbie okay?'

'Yes he's fine now.'

'Okay, Mrs White. I'll get my colleague to take a statement and a description of the car you saw. You haven't by any chance got the registration number, have you?'

'Well, I remember the first three numbers, five, eight, two, but I forgot the rest. I know there was a cee and a bee and another letter. I dow remember the order they was in though. I'm a bit dyslectic ya see.'

'I'm sure that will help us immensely, Mrs White,' Jack smiled. 'Thank you for coming in and thank you for the present.'

Saturday, 2pm

'The staff at the library all say Catherine left at five-thirty. She didn't appear upset about anything and was looking forward to her night out. She was an intelligent young woman who worked hard. No-one had a bad word to say against her.' Ted Bateman stood in the doorway of Jack's office and picked at the scab on his brow.

'All right, Ted. What about house to house?'

'Nothing, except Mrs White who saw the blue car. We're looking at CCTV footage from the library. It shows Catherine leaving at five-thirty-one. The next camera is near the shops, which is past the spot where the blue car was parked, but we're also looking at CCTV for weeks preceding her abduction. The car must be on camera somewhere along that road if he's been watching her. There's no sign of it on the footage we've looked at so far.'

'Perhaps he's been watching her on foot, which could mean he lives locally, or maybe it was a random opportunist. He almost hit me and I did think of going after him, but to be honest it was my own fault. I wanted to get home to change my wet clothes. Just think, she could have been lying on the back seat of that car just a few feet away from me.'

'I know. One of the team found a handkerchief in the road near to where the car was parked. I've sent it to forensics. It could be nothing at all to do with the crime but it's gone along with all the bottle-tops, fag ends and coke tins we found in and around the bin on the path to the park. There's four teams working house to house and Jones, Poole and three other constables are checking CCTV at the shops and houses along the route. I've got Constable Wallace and a couple of PCSOs are looking for combinations of the numbers and letters Mrs White gave you.'

'I've been through Lily's file again, Ted, and a Donald Smith said he'd seen a blue car parked near the college three or four times during the week she went missing. He sells newspapers from a kiosk on Newbury Road. It might be worth going to see him again. Send that young constable who needs a zip on his mouth round to see him. He's been talking non-stop about the post-mortem he went to the other day, telling everyone in the canteen that intestines look like fresh roe before you boil it. I don't think anyone who heard him will ever eat it again, including me.'

Ted Bateman chuckled and scratched his brow again. 'That's Joe Wallace, sir. I heard about that. Apparently the other new lad, Hadley, was next to him in the queue and he ran out the canteen and vomited in the hallway. The lads are calling them Wallace and Vomit now.'

'Are they? I can sympathise with the lad. Don't let it get out of hand, Ted. We don't want to put the new boys off.'

'No, I'll keep my eye on it. Just a bit of fun, that's all.'

'The car has to be our priority, Ted. Keep them at it till they find something.'

'Yes, sir.'

'Oh, and send Hadley to see me when he comes in. He's a friend of Catherine Bennett. I want to know just how close he is to her. When he spoke of her last night his eyes glassed over like a lovesick puppy. I might have to take him off the case.'

'Yes, sir.'

'Ted, your brow's bleeding.' Jack handed him a tissue. 'You ought to go and get that thing checked you know. You've had it a few weeks now, haven't you?' Ted's faced reddened. 'Yes, it's my own fault. I can't stop messing with it. Marge goes mad. She says it's an ulcer or something.'

'She's probably right. Just go and get it looked at, will you?'

'Yes I will. Do you fancy a pint in The Bull later?'

'Sorry, I'm going to visit my mother.'

'Say no more. Maybe another night.'

*

It had been a month since Jack had visited his mother at Bumble Cottage. Situated just outside Segmore in the small village of Coston, it reminded him so much of the cottage where he'd grown up in Riley Cross. The garden was in full bloom. A sea of yellow, pink and blue moved in a gentle breeze and the smell of newly cut grass tantalised his nostrils. He felt like the 'Bisto boy'. He remembered being very happy as a child when he played in the garden at Riley Cross.

Jack's ancestors were smugglers on the coast of Devon. His great, great, great grandfather, Jack O' Riley, was buried in the centre of the village and the grave was marked with a huge white cross, hence the name of the village came to be known as Riley Cross. The villagers had loved him for his generosity and made him mayor. He built the school and the church and made Riley Cross a better place to live.

Jack never mentioned his past to anyone. It was something that might cause him to get a bit of stick off the lads and DCI Murray. It was also the reason he'd dropped the 'O' from his name, much to the disapproval of his mother.

He left Riley Cross to go to university when he was eighteen. He remembered how strange it was to live in a town with people he didn't know. He'd known everyone in his village. Five years ago his mother had sold up and moved to the Midlands to be closer to her grandchild.

Jack's mother was in the kitchen when he went in. The smell of baking filled the air and made his mouth water. He could hear 'Flowers in the Rain' by the Move playing in the other room. For a second he was transported back to Riley Cross. His mother was a child of the sixties and he'd grown up with The Beatles, The Stones, Frankie Valli and Bob Dylan. Flower Power days. She lifted a tray from the oven and set it on the blue Formica work surface. Her kitchen was a throwback to the sixties as well.

'Oh, you remembered you have a mother, then?'

'I haven't come to argue.' Jack walked over to the kitchen table, pulled out a chair and sat down. He settled his eyes on the Welsh dresser across the room, which displayed his mother's collection of Portmeirion pottery. 'Another girl has gone missing in the area where Lily was taken.'

'Do you want tea?' His mother seemed to ignore his comment and poured boiling water into a flowery teapot.

'Yes please, and a piece of that cake if you don't mind.'

'It's carrot cake.' She brought a tray to the table and sat down. 'Do you think it's the same man who took Lily?' His mother's wavy, greying hair was cut short with a parting on the left side. She was still a good looking woman at sixty-five. She wore blue jeans, pink pumps and a pink shirt.

'There's a good chance it is, but nothing concrete. We have nothing to go on yet. But I've a feeling it's connected in some way to Lily's disappearance.'

'In the same area you say? I hope this doesn't mean he's killed my baby.'

'The thought had crossed my mind,' said Jack as he took a small bite from the hot cake. 'It's something I don't want to dwell on. I'll go insane. Where's Kitty?'

'She's at her writers' group. She has another six months at work.'

'Is she still headmistress at Dudstone High School?'

'Yes, thirty years now. She's looking forward to retiring though. She's so jealous of me being here all day.' His mother chuckled.

For a moment he saw the smile she always used to have before they lost Lily and his heart melted a bit. 'This cake is lovely. Can I have another piece?'

'Yes, but don't eat it hot, you'll get wind. Do you know anyone who might want to buy one of these? There's a few here to sell.' His mother pulled a DVD player from a plastic carrier bag.

Jack glanced at it then gave her a long look. 'I hope you're not selling knocked off stuff again, Mother.'

His mother ignored him and opened a cupboard door. 'There's a couple of flat screen TVs in here as well.'

Chapter Thirteen

Saturday

Michael was at his town house listening to Detective Chief Inspector Murray on the evening news channel. So, someone had clocked the Escort, but not the complete number plate. He knew they would probably find the full number on CCTV on the traffic light camera at the end of Broad Street. It was the route he took to leave the town. There were no cameras on the country lane back to Tipley, and there were three or four other lanes leading off that, so they wouldn't know which direction he'd taken after the left turn at the lights.

He'd found the old plates unopened in his grandmother's garage a few years back. She must have bought them but never used them. Anyone could have number plates made or buy them on the internet. If the police checked who bought them it wouldn't lead them to him, he was a child when they were bought and his grandmother had sold that car years ago.

No matter how much he tried to reason with

himself there was a nagging doubt in his mind. He'd made a mistake using them again. Maybe he'd pushed his luck too far this time. He just hoped Riley wouldn't find a connection. He owned a red Ford Focus, which he used when he came to his house. It was legally taxed, insured and registered to him in his new name. He would have to get some more plates for the Audi and the Escort or make them himself in the workshop at the back of the manor.

As far as anyone else was concerned he was a respectable member of the community. Philip, Jack-of-all-trades, or Michael, computer wizard. He had documents for both of them.

When he left the children's home his first stop had been his father's solicitors, Forbes and Waterman. They'd contacted him a few weeks before his eighteenth birthday to tell him they held his father's will. He owned properties worth over three million pounds and had two million pounds in other investments. He'd researched various methods of bone lengthening used throughout Europe and had found a private clinic in Dublin that could give him the treatment he needed. He walked out of the solicitors a wealthy man, he cashed in the investments, opened three bank accounts, then headed straight for Dublin. He lived there in a rented house for three years while he had his treatment. He changed his name by deed poll before his treatment began.

Private clinics weren't that fussy about what name you used if you had plenty of money. Celebrities did it all the time. He'd been shocked when he spied on his father and saw who walked down the cellar with him. A well-known British singer, who swore he'd never had plastic surgery on his face and an actress from one of the top American soaps, were regular visitors. He knew all their secrets. The newspapers would have a field day if he opened his mouth and there would be a lot of embarrassed celebrities trying to lie their way out of the truth.

The clinic in Dublin used the Ilizarov method. This involved using an external fixator consisting of rings, rods and Kirshner wires, all made of stainless steel. It was attached to the top and bottom of the bone and worked by stretching the bone little by little, causing new bone growth where it was stretched. The metal frame was kept in place until the new bone was strong enough to bear his weight. This process took several months and sometimes had to be repeated. The consultant told him there would probably still be a difference in the length of his legs. The treatment was successful but his left leg was still an inch shorter, which left him with a slight limp.

All he needed was an extra sole on his shoe and the limp was gone. But he'd used it to good advantage. Anyone who'd seen him at the library would report a blond haired man with spectacles and a limp. Michael did not wear spectacles, his hair was dark brown, he was as handsome as his father, he was the spit of him, even though he didn't like to admit it, and he no longer had a visible limp. It was all a charade, which he kept up when he went in to see the girls.

He bought his shoes online and added the extra sole himself. He didn't want to be measured for a 'special shoe' that was designed for cripples. He'd had enough of that during his miserable childhood when his father and the children's home had forced him to wear one. It was a boot with a huge sole and two sizes smaller than the boot on his right foot. It screamed, 'Look at me! I'm a cripple!'

While he was having his treatment he enrolled on an Open University degree in computer maintenance and programming. He got a first class with honours and glowing references from his tutors. To fill in the rest of the time he taught himself plumbing, car mechanics, electronics and passed his driving test. He absorbed knowledge like a sponge and had a photographic memory. His job, which he only did part time, was going out to companies to install and upgrade their computer systems.

It was well paid, even though he didn't need the money. Working for this company guaranteed employees' immediate respectability. Fast Bytes Technology was the company to be with if you were into computers. The company had expanded threefold in the last two years and Michael was one of their valued employees. He never had to clock in or go to the office. His worksheet was sent weekly via email.

He arrived at a place where all the equipment had been sent on before him. All he had to do was put it together.

He hadn't seen Jack Riley yet. According to the papers he was the one who'd been in the park, the one who had been within a whisker of catching him. He was so panic stricken he hadn't noticed it was Jack who almost bounced off the bonnet of the Escort. He was there after all. He thought he might like to pay him a visit, torment him some more, perhaps leave him something of his precious little girl before he got rid of her.

He opened a drawer and took out the girl's bag. Inside were two keys on a ring, which were probably for the doors of the flats, but the inspector had changed the locks when the girl went missing, so they were no good to him. There was also a purse, a student ID card, a make-up bag, a comb and the ring he'd taken from her finger. 'Yes, that will do nicely,' he said to himself, as he picked up the ring.

It was time to go back to feed them. He never gave them too much food. He didn't want them to be strong enough to fight him, besides girls should be petite and delicate, like angels. Riley's girl was beginning to look haggard. She looked less and less like Rebecca every day. How could he have made such a stupid mistake? She was the serpent in disguise. His Rebecca had been pure.

If she hadn't been carrying his child, she would be in the shed now. But he had to see the child, to see if it came out like the other one, the one he kept upstairs. He would also have to feed him. The only reason he'd kept the child alive was to see if he could mend the crooked legs it was born with. It was a kind of experiment for him.

He'd made the leg apparatus in his father's workshop. When he succeeded he would show the world what a brilliant surgeon he was.

When he got back to the manor he went to see the child. It was in the room where its mother had died. Trays of rat poison littered the floor. The room smelt of urine and faeces. Michael put a mask over his nose and mouth. The boy looked up at the ceiling with dull grey eyes. It hardly ever cried, he was grateful for that at least. A drip was attached to his arm and he was held down with leather straps. Metal rods were attached to both legs, making it impossible for him to move, even without the straps.

Various tubes were attached to his body and he was naked except for a cloth, loosely wrapped round the lower half of his body to catch waste. Michael inspected the cloth and changed it. He put the soiled one in a plastic bag, ready to be burned with the garden rubbish. Then he attached a liquid food bottle to a tube in the child's stomach.

He adjusted the screws on the steel rods and the child cried out in pain.

*

The girl was awake. She thought about her tasks. Every day she had to wash her sheet, towel and pillow case in the sink, then her pants and gown. She hung them to dry on the cast iron radiator. She had three of everything, which were rotated each day. One set to wear, one set to wash, one set in the drawer.

The first thing he did when he came in the room was feel the washing to make sure it was wet. If he saw a speck of dirt on it, he would punish her with a slap across the face, or a kick to the shins. She was still bruised from his last assault.

Everything had to be washed in the sink with a bar of carbolic soap. She did this task as quickly as she could and counted all the time, because she couldn't catch the drips in her bowl and she must keep track of time. Then she swept and mopped the floor and cleaned the sink and toilet. This had been her routine for more than two years.

The Doctor inspected everything. She was always

terrified when he came in case he found something wrong. The only time her mind was calm was when she slept, and even then sometimes nightmares invaded that little bit of peace she had, and the face of the devil had the eyes of the Doctor.

*

Catherine had been awake hours. She heard someone moving around in another room, a toilet flushed. She was sure it wasn't the Doctor. The last time he'd gone out she'd heard the singing again, the same song, the soft voice. She remembered the film now. It was *Mighty Joe Young*, the forerunner to *King Kong*.

She was going to call out the next time the Doctor went out. She wanted the other girl to know she wasn't alone in her torment.

The Doctor had given her a list of things to do and left a new bar of soap on the sink top. She got out of bed and started to clean the sink. She was still dizzy from the drugs he'd given her. She couldn't think straight. Was this a dream? What about the other noises too, besides the singing? There was a baby crying. She wondered if she'd really heard it. She wasn't sure. She knew that drugs could make you hallucinate and hear sounds. Maybe she hadn't heard anything at all. When she reached under the sink to get the mop bucket a glint of white caught her eye. She bent down to take a closer look. There was a large crack round the water outlet pipe. She could see daylight.

Chapter Fourteen

Jack had eaten his Sunday lunch at the Bull and Bear for the last two years. The cosy town centre pub had real log fires in the winter and a tidy garden out the back for hot summer nights. The landlord, Mat, valued his customers and regularly put on a pot of grey peas and bacon free of charge. Jack kept his eye on the blackboard for the date when the free supper was advertised. On these nights a local singer would come to entertain, also free of charge, so long as Mat and the customers provided him with plenty of free beer. Jack welcomed the company and sing along on these nights, it helped him to cope with the heartbreak of losing his daughter.

Mat had teased Jack about his southern accent when he first came to Dudstone and had called him a foreigner. After almost nineteen years in the place, he still playfully called him "the foreigner".

Jack tended to eat out a lot since Lily had gone. He found no joy in cooking meals they'd prepared and cooked together. The pub was across the road from his flat and although the menu hardly changed, it was handy. He could also have a couple of pints and walk home. It was usually full of colleagues and firemen. The fire station was down the road from the police station and the men often drank together.

He'd just finished eating when his mobile phone rang. 'Riley here.'

'Hello, Jack, it's Marge Bateman. I think you should know Ted's in hospital. That sore on his brow could be cancer.'

'I'm sorry to hear that, Marge. I kept telling him to get it checked.'

'He went this morning because it was bleeding all night. They took him to Conley, Jack. They're doing some tests, they've got better facilities there. I'm on my way there now.'

'I hope he'll be okay, Marge. Keep me informed.'

'I will, Jack. Bye.'

As Jack put his phone back in his pocket it rang again. He looked at the caller ID and sighed. 'Riley here, sir,' he answered and wondered if Murray had also had a call from Marge Bateman.

'Jack, an hour ago two walkers found a body on the Limes Nature Reserve. All I know is it's female. I'll meet you there. Have you heard about Bateman?'

'Yes, sir.'

'Just when we're short staffed, as well.'

'You can't blame him for being ill, sir.'

'It's bad timing, Jack. Superintendent Middleton is giving me earache about it. Everybody's stretched to the limit and they're on about cutting back on recruiting more officers and getting more volunteers. I'll tell you something. Another six months and they can have my job as well. I'm getting out while I'm still standing. Anyway, I'll bring DS Morgan along with me. You can meet your new partner.'

*

The Limes Nature Reserve was a dividing line between two council estates. One aptly named the Limes Estate and the other the Castle Estate because it was built near Dudstone Castle. The Limes was so-called because it was an area where limestone had been quarried over a century ago.

A few years back, in the nineteen-sixties the area had been subject to subsidence due to the underground mines and people on the Limes Estate had woken up to find their back gardens had disappeared and huge holes had taken their place. A lot of blasting was done on the nature reserve to fill in the holes and make it safe. Ten yards down the road from the entrance to the nature reserve stood the local pub, The Quarryman's Arms.

Uniformed officers were having a hard time holding back the drinkers, who had spilled out onto the car park. The people on this estate had had it rough. Many were unemployed. Large families lived in small houses and the estate provided a steady flow of burglars and car thieves, who were regularly hauled before the local constabulary. If the body was a local girl, vigilantes would be out.

When Jack had first moved to Dudstone someone had exposed himself to a young lad from the Limes Estate. It hadn't taken the locals long to hunt the beast down and serve out their own kind of justice. He was a man who lived on the Castle Estate, who had previous convictions for exposing himself on the nature reserve. He never walked again, or exposed himself. No-one was arrested for what happened to him.

Jack pulled up outside the warden's office at the nature reserve. There were several other police vehicles there and a group of officers looking towards the shale pathway that led to the reserve. It was cordoned off with tape and the SOC team was taking equipment into the warden's office. He caught a glimpse of Gwen O'Brien, the police forensic pathologist, in her white overalls as she went into the office with a box. He got out the car and walked unsteadily towards the group.

This body could be Lily. It could also be Catherine. He felt bile rise in his throat, his dinner threatening to come up any minute. He forced it back down and patted his coat pockets for a cigarette. He didn't have any.

'How ya doin', Mr Riley?' came a voice from the crowd that sounded familiar.

Jack looked to the side.

Joey Coombs lifted up a pint glass and smiled.

'Hello Joey,' Jack replied as he passed the dozen or so drinkers.

Murray stepped out of the group to meet him. 'The body's six yards in, just off the track in a clump of bushes.' A flame-haired young woman appeared at his shoulder. 'This is DS. Sandy Morgan. She'll be working with you while Bateman's away.'

The young woman smiled and nodded. Jack thought she looked a bit young to be a DS.

'Pleased to meet you, sir.' DS Morgan offered her hand.

'Same here,' replied Jack as he shook her outstretched hand.

'Get your gear on, Sandy,' said Murray.

Jack looked up the path, the colour drained from his face.

Murray looked at him. 'I'll go and have a quick look. You wait here, Jack.'

'Are you okay, sir?' DS Morgan asked, as she tightened a band to keep the flaming hair under control.

'I'm fine.' He pulled a pair of latex gloves from his coat pocket, tried to put one on his left hand and tore it.

DS Morgan pulled another pair from her bag and passed them to him. 'I always keep half a dozen pairs handy.'

'Good for you,' said Jack. 'Always prepared, like a girl guide.'

'That's boy scout, sir.'

'What is?'

'It's their motto. Boy scouts be prepared.'

'Are you always so nit-picky, DS Morgan?'

'I'm afraid so, sir,' she smiled.

Murray returned. 'I don't think you should go there, Jack.'

Jack's legs buckled.

Murray put out a hand to steady him. 'I can't tell who it is. Her face is almost gone.' DS Morgan looked confused.

'Jack's daughter was taken two years ago,' Murray explained.

'I have to see her,' said Jack. 'I need to know.'

'You can wait for DNA. That's if they can get any. I don't think you should see what's up there. It's certainly not Catherine Bennett. She's wrapped in plastic sheets and with the hot weather we've had she's badly decomposed. Wait and see what Gwen says.'

'I'll have a look, sir,' DS Morgan said.

'Help yourself. Don't get in the way of the SOC team.'

'I won't, sir. I do know the procedure.' She turned to Jack. 'Is there anything you want me to look for that's a distinguishing feature on your daughter?'

Jack felt his stomach lurch. 'Her ears were pierced and she wore a signet ring her grandmother had given her for her thirteenth birthday. She never took it off.'

'Which finger? Which hand, sir?'

'Third finger, right hand,' said Jack frustrated as he peeled off the latex gloves. 'But I doubt it will be there.'

'There will be an indent on her finger if she wore the ring for a long period of time, sir,' said DS Morgan as she headed off up the path.

'She looks like a kid,' said Murray, 'but she seems

to know what she's doing.'

'She's just following the text books,' said Jack.

Murray cut him a look. 'Well, for god's sake, give her a chance, Jack! We all have to follow text books at some time or another. She's been with Yorkshire division for three years, and we all know they have the best up there. I called you in because you're my most senior officer. If, god forbid, it turns out to be Lily, you're off the case, Jack. I can't afford to have you going round threatening innocent people again.'

He rubbed his stomach and burped loudly. 'Fucking acid!'

*

Catherine bent down to have a closer look at the hole under the sink. A piece of mortar about an inch wide and three inches long lay on the bottom of the cupboard behind the bucket. She kneeled down and leaned into the cupboard to feel round the pipe for more loose pieces. The hole was big enough for her to see grass. She put her fingers in and tried to loosen some more. It moved slightly. She looked round for something to use as a tool. The Doctor always gave her a plastic fork to eat her food and he was careful to take it away when she'd finished. 'What use would it be for anything else other than eating?' she murmured to herself. Her eyes rested on the mop in the corner. Perhaps she could prod the bricks with the handle.

A door closed. A few seconds later a car door slammed and the engine started up. He was going out. The girl opened her eyes. She licked her lips. The cold sore was healing, but her ankles were still swollen and there was an ache in her back that wouldn't go away.

She laid on her back, her right side, her left side, it still ached.

She sat up and began to sing, 'Beautiful Dreamer', wake unto me, Starlight and dewdrops are waiting for thee; Sounds of the rude world, heard in the day, lulled by the moonlight have all…'

'Hello! Hello! Who's there?'

The girl stopped singing. Someone had called out.

*

Michael parked on the underground car park in the centre of Dudstone. He knew Jack Riley lived in the flat above the tailor's, it had been well publicised when his daughter had gone missing. He also knew that right now Jack would be eating his lunch in the Bull and Bear, which was less than twenty yards away across the road.

But he loved the thrill of danger. The only obstacle in his way might be the old woman who lived in the other flat. He wasn't too concerned about her though.

Today he'd got long ginger hair and wore a blue boiler suit. The I.D. badge pinned to his chest read PHIL. He glanced across the road towards the police station, a feeling of power surged through his veins. This was going to be so easy, he could feel the beginning of an erection. The door to the flats was at the side of the shop. He pressed the buzzer for flat two and waited.

After half a minute or so, he pressed the buzzer again. There was a crackling sound, then a gruff. 'Hello, who's there?'

'I'm here to check the electrics,' he answered. 'Mr

Riley asked me to come.'

'He didn't tell me,' the voice replied.

'Oh. Well, I'll come back another time if you want to take the risk of a burnout.'

'A burnout? What do you mean?'

'Mr Riley phoned me this morning and said there was a burning smell on the landing. He wanted me to check yours first, he doesn't want you to be at risk. But I'll come back tomorrow if it's not convenient.'

'You'd better come in,' said the voice. 'Push the door when you hear the click.' The door clicked. He pushed it open and went in.

*

'Well, sir. I think I can be pretty certain in saying she's not your daughter or Catherine Bennett. Her ears weren't pierced and the body's decomposed too much to be Catherine. The flesh is falling off in chunks. Rats have eaten her eyes.'

The words had barely left DS Morgan's mouth when Jack ran across the car park and threw up in the bushes.

'I think it will be okay for you to have a look, sir. It's very interesting.' DS Morgan called after him.

'You make it sound like a bloody work of art!' Jack shouted and retched again.

'Are you okay, Riley?' Murray trotted up behind him, beads of sweat bubbling on his creased brow. He pulled a handkerchief from his trouser pocket and mopped his face and head. 'I know this has been hard for you, but I want you to get focused on this and give the girl some encouragement. She's good at her job. She works with enthusiasm.'

'I can see she delights in it,' Jack replied.

'You okay, sir?' DS Morgan bobbed in front of him with a bottle of water. 'This might help.'

'Thank you DS Morgan. That's very kind of you.' He gave her a false smile, took the bottle of water, then turned to Murray and whispered, 'Is that encouraging enough?'

Gwen O' Brien and some of her team came out of the warden's office with boxes of samples from the crime scene. She handed her box to a colleague when she saw Jack and went over to him.

'Are you ok, Jack?' She put a hand on his shoulder, leaned in close and looked at him as if he was a child with a grazed knee.

'I'll be ok in a minute.' Jack touched her hand. 'It's a bit of a shock.'

'Come and sit with me in my car for a few minutes, you're shaking like a leaf.'

Chapter Fifteen

The girl wasn't sure what to do. She wondered if the voice was a trap. Perhaps the Doctor was testing her to see if she'd call back.

'Hello! What's your name? I'm Catherine Bennett! Hello! Please answer me!'

If this was a test, it would mean the Doctor was using another girl to call to her.

He was smart though, it would be something he would do to trick her. But the scream she heard, surely that wasn't a trick.

'Hello! I'm Lily! Lily Riley!'

'Hello, Lily! I remember reading about you in the paper! Your father's a policeman, isn't he?'

'Yes! How long have you been here, Catherine?'

'A few days I think! He grabbed me on my way from work! I'm not really sure. He gives me drugs to make me sleep.'

'It seems like I've been here all my life. It has to be two years or more.'

'Yes, it is, Lily. It's July, two-thousand and thirteen now. Do you know why he's kidnapped us?'

'He says he's looking for a bride, who must be pure and perfect. Then he does terrible things. Torture. Starving. Beatings. I don't want to scare you, Catherine, but he's done unthinkable things to me and made me suffer terrible pain. He's a mad man.'

'Oh, my god!' Catherine sobbed.

'You must do as he says, Catherine. I'm still here after all this time. Just try to be obedient and please him. I'm telling you these things so that you can save yourself. If you do anything he considers disrespectful to him he will beat and torture you.'

'Lily I don't want to die!'

'You won't if you do as he says. Don't ever laugh at him. Don't let him see you frown. Don't tell him if you have a boyfriend. And don't ever let him catch you talking to me. He expects total obedience and submission. When he brings you food try to save some because he won't feed you every day. You will always be hungry. Put some bread between the sheets in the drawer. He never looks there.'

'Thank you, Lily.'

'What's going on in the world? Are they still looking for me?'

'It hasn't been on the news for quite some time now, but I'm sure your father will never give up looking for you.'

*

The old woman was on the landing when he went up.

'The electric boxes are in that cupboard,' she pointed. 'I was just going to make tea. Would you like a cup?'

'That would be lovely,' he replied, as he opened the cupboard door.

As soon as the old woman had gone back in her flat he took the ring from his pocket, wiped it with his gloved hand and pushed it under the door to Jack's flat. He smiled. Riley was going to be shocked when he found it. He heard the clatter of teacups and looked round the open door. It wouldn't take long to do her. He had a lovely sharp scalpel in his bag and Riley wouldn't be back for a while. He picked up his bag, went in and closed the door.

Phil Clarke, Electrical Engineer, was about to do a bit of overtime. It was a shame the real Phil had been dressed as a tramp and found dead on a park bench in Dublin a few years back. His face had been obliterated by acid. He was buried as John Doe.

Michael and Phil had shared the house in Dublin. The unfortunate young man had been an orphan, just like him.

*

Jack sat in Gwen's car for ten minutes. The shock of finding the body had hit him hard and it took a while for him to stop shaking.

'It's not Lily,' Gwen said as she passed him the cigarette she was smoking. 'I can imagine how you must have felt when you heard about the body though. I felt a bit shaken myself. But I've seen her, Jack, and I can assure you it's not Lily. I went with her to get her ears pierced. This girl doesn't have piercings.'

'The new DS. told me that. I'm always waiting for the bad news, Gwen. It's like eternal torture. I hardly sleep.'

'I know. I'd be the same if it was my child who was missing. You have to hold it together, Jack. Don't give up hope of finding her alive. Come on, we need to get back to work.'

*

'There was another missing girl case about a year before your daughter went missing, sir.' DS Morgan sat on the corner of Jack's desk sipping coffee from a polystyrene cup. 'Amelia Stevens. She was twenty, blond, petite, just like Lily and Catherine. Do you think there's a connection?'

'Do you mind?' Jack moved round his desk to get papers she was sitting on.

'Must you keep up this constant chatter DS Morgan?'

'Oh, sorry,' DS Morgan stood up and moved out of his way.

'They're all creased now.' He held the crumpled folder under her nose. 'Do you intend to park your backside on my desk all day?'

'I'm trying to be helpful, sir. I think the dead girl is Amelia Stevens.'

'What makes you think that?'

'I'm familiar with the case. I read the file on her when I was in Yorkshire. She had a star tattooed on her left ear lobe. I'm just waiting to hear from the pathologist. The position the body was in prevented me from looking at the scene. There were body fluids leaking everywhere and flesh hanging off like pieces of meat. They wouldn't move her head in case it fell off. The stench was out of this world and maggots wriggling up her...'

'For god's sake! Do you have to be so graphic DS Morgan? I've already thrown my breakfast and dinner up, anything else that comes up will be from yesterday.'

Someone tapped on the door and opened it. 'There's a lady from the library here to see you, sir.' Constable Wallace stood in the doorway. 'I think she's got information about the Catherine Bennett kidnapping. I can take a statement if you're busy sir, or...'

'Take a statement, Wallace. We're waiting to hear from the pathologist. Are the computers working now?'

DS Morgan threw Jack a sideways glance and smiled.

'Yes, sir. The technician said the monitors need replacing. I've found the car on CCTV and I think I've got the full registration now. It was on the traffic lights at the end of Broad Street.'

'Well done, lad. Run it through the database to find out who owns it. It's an old registration. Get one of the PCSOs to help you.'

'Yes, sir.'

'I remember the Stevens girl. It was East Yorkshire wasn't it?' Jack said, as the door closed.

'Yes. I went to help with it, but she was never found. She was taken in the early hours. She'd been to a nightclub, got split up from her friends and vanished. A witness said she saw her get in a black car, which she thought was a taxi, but no-one else came forward. No taxi driver.'

'I'll have a look at the file. Was the witness checked out?'

'Of course she was. We couldn't rely on her evidence though, she was out of her face on coke.'

'Don't you think it's a bit suspicious that the taxi driver didn't come forward to clear his name?'

'Yes. We traced every driver who worked for local taxi firms. They all had good alibis. They were either with a fare or at the depot. Everyone was accounted for. I remember how anxious they were to clear their names. None of them wanted to be associated with girls disappearing after the 'Lost Girls of Larchester' case. So we came to the conclusion that it wasn't a taxi or the kidnapper pretended to be a taxi driver. Or the witness was hallucinating. The case went cold. We had nothing to go on. I returned to Yorkshire and heard nothing else. I've got a close friend in the force. I can ask him if there were any more developments.'

'Wasn't there any CCTV outside the club? It could have been a taxi from another town.'

'There was a camera but it was broken. There's footage from inside the club. You can see Amelia dancing with another young woman.'

'What about the surrounding streets? If she got in a taxi it's going to be on camera either coming into the town or going out.'

'I think someone did do some checks but didn't find anything. Do you think we should look again?'

'If the body is Amelia, it will have to be reopened.' Jack smiled. 'Maybe you'll see your close friend again. What's this 'Lost Girls' case you mentioned?'

'My god! Where have you been the last twenty years? Don't you remember the missing students from Larchester? Nineteen-ninety to ninety-eight? Eight students went missing. Never been found. Scared the shit out of me. One of them lived a few doors away from my house. Sandra Tromans. I was just joining the force when the last one went missing. When Amelia went missing the newspapers dragged it all up again.'

'Oh, yes. I remember now. I joined in ninety-one. Spent my first two years in Manchester, then moved here. You don't think it's the same bloke who's started up again, do you?'

'You never know. They were all students like Lily and Catherine. I'd have to compare the cases to the more recent ones.'

'Amelia wasn't a student.'

'No, she was a bit of a drop-out. Got in with the wrong crowd. The kidnapper could have been desperate for his kick and chosen the first girl he saw, especially after a long period of inactivity.'

'He could have been in prison during that time. I mean, would he suddenly cease to kidnap girls if it was a compulsion?'

'I don't know. A new book is written for every killer or kidnapper. They're all unique in what makes them do what they do and the way they do it. Murder can be an addiction just like cocaine or sex.'

'Fifteen years is a long time.'

'Yes, it is. I think he's a different person, maybe a copycat. That isn't unknown with mass murders or kidnappings.'

'Murders committed in a way that has been established by a previous killer. Like Jack the Ripper.'

'Yes. There was a spate of similar killings after The Ripper, that's when the term "copycat" was coined.'

'And there have been many more since. Nineteen-ninety-eight you joined. That makes you around thirty-six then?' Jack smiled.

'I'm admitting nothing without my solicitor present,' replied DS Morgan.

*

When Michael returned to the manor he heard Catherine calling out as he opened the door. He opened the Bible on the table and read from Jeremiah, '..if it does evil in My sight by not obeying My voice, then I will think better of the good with which I had promised to bless it.' He went to the cupboard in the lounge, opened the drawer and picked up the wooden club. He would have to discipline her now. She could make as much noise as she wanted, no-one would hear her. He just loved to see the fear in her eyes.

She was sitting on the bed when he went in. Just look at her, pretending innocence, he thought, as he limped across the room with a syringe held in the hand behind his back. As soon as he was close enough he stuck it in her arm.

'You've been disobedient, Catherine. You've been calling out and I specifically told you that noise was not allowed. Now you have to be punished. Just a few simple rules and you can't obey them. You are just like the others.' His voice was firm, his face blank. 'You've spoilt all my plans now. Everything I've done for you. It's all ruined! Why couldn't you be the one who gave me total obedience? The money I've spent on your beautiful clothes for our union! Two days! And you have betrayed me already!' He shouted. His right eye began to twitch.

Catherine's head was fuzzy. The Doctor blurred in front of her.

'You will have no food today!' He screamed in her face.

She was too weak to answer. Her head spun as if she'd just stepped off a roundabout in the park. Round and round.

'I can't tell you how much it hurts me to do this to you, Catherine, but it's for your own good. I have to test you now.' He pulled her pants down and pushed his fingers inside her. 'If you can't be obedient in mind, you can't be pure in body.'

*

Lily jumped up as a blood curdling scream echoed through the building.

The Doctor shouted obscenities as he tortured Catherine.

Another scream.

Lily shook and curled up on the bed. She covered

her ears with her hands. He must have heard them talking. It was only a matter of time before he came to her.

Michael could hear Catherine's muffled sobs as he wrote in the book: *I thought she was the one who would be perfect, the one who would be submissive, but she is the same as the other two. The sly bitch! I pushed my fingers into her and found no resistance inside. Someone has been there before.*

'You dirty fucking slut!' he shouted. Then wrote again: *She is impure. She has to go. My search is not over.* He closed the book.

'It's for your own good,' he heard his father's voice. 'You soiled your bedclothes again. You back-answered your mother. Obedience is the word. Now you must take your punishment like a man. If you cry out, you will suffer more.'

He would have to concentrate more on Goldilocks. He knew she would be pure. She'd asked him to put up his photo in the chat room. He would have to find a suitable one. A good looking fourteen-year-old-boy. He'd been a good looking fourteen-year-old-boy and the staff at the children's home had taken many pictures of him. He would look for one. But now it was time to clean out the shed and make room for the next one.

Chapter Sixteen

Monday morning

Jack woke up, showered, shaved and put on a clean
shirt and tie. He decided to tidy himself up, to stay on
the boss's good side for a while. He also planned on
going to see his mother again to warn her about the
stolen goods and her association with a certain man
by the name of Eddie Taylor, also known as Fisheye.
He knew it wouldn't be easy. Things hadn't been right
with them since Lily had gone and he felt as if he was
treading on eggshells whenever they were together.

From the age of fourteen Jack had worked on the
fishing boats during the summer holidays. At sixteen
he worked weekends washing up in the Fisherman's
Knot pub until he finished school and was ready for
university. All the money he earned was put in a bank
account and when he left for university his mother
handed it all back to him, plus an extra ten thousand
pounds. He never asked where the money came from,
but had suspicions it was not honestly earned.

His grandfather was a rogue and made regular trips
across the channel to France to bring in whiskey and

cigarettes, which he sold to pubs and clubs along the coast. He was still dabbling where he shouldn't at eighty-five years of age.

Jack always thought his mother was hard on him because she blamed him for his father's absence. The father he had never known or seen. Then three years ago she spilled the beans. His father had not been a soldier. He was just a friend she knew who she asked to make her pregnant. There was no great love between them.

Those early tales she spun about his father being killed in a bomb blast in Ulster had been a lie. She'd burst his bubble good and proper and at the time he thought he could never forgive her for all the deceit. Yet, she accused him of being a bad parent.

*

As he closed his door, Miss Baker's cat meowed and rubbed herself round his ankles.

'How did you get out, Polly? Come on, back you go.' He picked up the cat and noticed Miss Baker's door was slightly ajar. He pushed it open and went inside. 'Stella? Are you there?'

He looked in the kitchen. There was a tray set with two cups and a plate of biscuits. The teapot was full, but cold. 'Stella, are you okay?' Jack knew the old woman hardly left the flat except for visits to the doctor. He tapped on the bedroom door. 'Are you in there?' He opened the bedroom door and looked in. What he saw made him reel backwards and fall into the hall. The old woman was lying naked on the bed. She was tied to the bed by her hands and feet and covered in blood.

As Jack fumbled in his coat pocket to get his phone, he heard her faintly call his name.

'Dudstone Police Station. This is Police Constable Wallace. How can I help you?'

'Riley here, Wallace. Get an ambulance and a team round to my place now! Someone has attacked Miss Baker!' Jack shook as he bent over her.

'Jack,' she whispered again. 'Help me, Jack.'

He took her hand. 'You're going to be okay. I'm here.' The buzzer sounded and he moved to press the button to let the team in.

Murray appeared in the doorway of Jack's flat. 'I'm sorry about this, Jack. It must be devastating for you to find her like this. When did you last see her?' It was business as usual for Murray.

'I'm not sure. Perhaps a day, two days,' said Jack. 'What kind of animal does that to an old woman?'

'A fucking insane one.' Murray came in the room and sat on the couch next to Jack. 'If you want some time off it's okay.'

'Time off? No thanks. I'm going to catch the bastard who did this. And then I'm going to kill him.'

'Don't tell me things like that.' Murray stood up. 'They're not holding out much hope for her in there, Jack. She's lost a lot of blood. You go and visit Bateman and I'll sort things here. I'll get them to look at CCTV outside. Have you no cameras in the building?'

'No, sir.'

'Well I think you should get some. It might be too

late for the poor woman in there, but it could be you next, Jack. Did you touch anything in the bedroom?'

'What kind of a question is that?'

'A crime scene question.'

'What?'

'Ridiculous as it seems. Close male contacts. The tray was set for two people. She was expecting someone.'

'It wasn't me... my prints will be all over the flat. I'm always popping in for a cup of tea and I decorated her bedroom last year for god's sake!'

'There's a team checking CCTV in the street. I'm sure we'll see who came in.'

'It must have been yesterday when I was at the crime scene. I noticed the door open this morning and the cat was out on the landing.'

'While you're here, I have some more news. You won't believe who owns the number plate Constable Wallace was checking.'

'Who is it?' Jack asked.

'Claude Benson,' said Murray.

'Benson, as in scrap merchant?'

'The one and only,' said Murray. 'I've sent a constable to bring him in.'

*

Ted Bateman was in a side ward. He was sitting up in bed reading a book when Jack opened the door.

'Sorry about this, Jack.'

'I told you to get it checked ages ago. What do the doctors say about it?' Jack sat in the bedside chair.

'They're doing some tests. The prognosis is good. The doc thinks it's a pre-cancerous growth and he can cure it. How's the case going? I heard you've found a body.'

'Yes. She was found on the Limes Nature Reserve. I'm going to the mortuary later. There's something else, Ted. Someone came to the flats and attacked Miss Baker. She's barely alive.'

'My god, Jack! The poor woman. Do you think it's anything to do with the disappearance of the girls?'

'I think it has something to do with Catherine's disappearance.'

'Does Miss Baker have a key to your flat?'

'Yes, but it was still on her key ring in her bag. I don't think anyone went in my flat. Nothing seems amiss. I'm hoping she'll be able to tell me something if she survives surgery. There was so much blood I couldn't see how bad the wounds were. There were two cups set for tea. She let whoever did this in. I'm wondering if she knew her attacker. I've never known anyone visit her. I'm absolutely devastated, Ted. She must have been terrified lying there on her own all night.'

'I hope she'll be okay. The poor woman. Are there any other developments with the Bennett case?'

'There's a new DS. come down from Yorkshire to help with the case. Sandy Morgan. I was expecting a bloke and she turns up, looking like a school girl, acting like a girl guide. Miss Know-All. Got a head of hair like a fireball and a mouth that runs off a battery. She babbles constantly about blood and gore as if she's a bloody vampire and her mouth's watering.'

Ted laughed. 'You like her then?'

'Well, there's room for improvement,' Jack smiled. 'Anyway. One of the librarians came in and gave a statement to Wallace. She said a fair haired young man with spectacles and a limp had been coming to the library two or three times a week for about a month, but he hasn't been there since Catherine went missing. I've asked her to call us if he turns up and put a description out to all units to be on the look-out for him. DCI Murray's giving another press conference today. I think he'll be appealing for any information on the young man. We also found out who owns the registration plate that Mrs White gave us. It's Claude Benson the scrap dealer. Murray's sent a car to bring him in. I'll let you know the outcome when I've spoken to him, but I don't think Claude had anything to do with the kidnapping.'

'It's three girls now then? Do you think they're all connected, Jack?'

'Three girls but only one body. She's been positively identified as Amelia Stevens. Went missing in East Yorkshire, January two thousand and ten, fourteen months before Lily. Apparently she'd left home three months prior to her disappearance and was living in a squat. A girl who shared a room with her reported her missing when she didn't show up at the squat for a few days. Her parents also put in a missing person's report when she hadn't called them and her phone was switched off when they tried to call her. I think we might be dealing with a very intelligent psychopath, Ted, and yes I think there's a connection but we have to prove it. The DNA on the handkerchief found at the scene where Catherine was abducted is that of a white male aged twenty-five to thirty, with dark hair and blue eyes There was hair from his nose, skin, mucous, sweat and clothes fibres on it. There were also traces of chloroform. We're hoping to find something to connect him to the dead girl as well. There were fibres and hairs on the plastic sheet she was wrapped in. I think they found some blood as well. If we do find anything, it might rule out the young man with the blond hair.'

Ted coughed. 'Not necessarily, Jack. He could have been wearing a disguise.'

'That's a fair point, Ted. I have considered he might have worn a wig.'

'Well, if he's as clever as you think he is, he would do something like that to lay a false trail, wouldn't he? He might not even realise he dropped the handkerchief. Many killers dress up or use objects to disguise themselves. You only have to think about Ted Bundy and his plaster cast.'

'If he's that clever he wouldn't have dropped the handkerchief. He might have planted it to implicate someone else. There are countless possibilities. But if he's trying to implicate someone else, sooner or later he'll slip up.'

'Did Wallace have any luck finding Donald Smith?'

'Yes. He died last year. In his statement he says he saw a small blue car in the area two or three times the week Lily went missing, but he couldn't tell us the make or model. I was hoping to show him some photographs to see if he could identify it as an Escort. I can't understand why we didn't pursue it further at the time.'

'You had a breakdown, remember? And you were taken off the case.'

'Yes, I know. Who took over the investigation?'

'Jones, I think.'

'Mickey! Well, maybe that explains why Mr Smith wasn't shown photographs at the time. He just couldn't be arsed.'

'I don't think it would have made much difference to the enquiries, Jack, we didn't have a registration number to go on.'

'Mickey makes my piss boil, Ted. I could knock that grin off his face.'

'Now Jack. You know why that is. He only had one date with her and you can't forget it.'

'Why would she go out with an arsehole?'

'Because you were chasing a certain D.C. at the time. Remember?'

'Jon had only been dead six months. I didn't think she'd be interested in going out with anyone else. The idiot had only been here two months. I thought she'd got more taste.'

'Gwen's her own woman, Jack. She does what she pleases. One date and she dropped him. You have to get over it.'

'Yes you're right, as usual. I'm off to the mortuary to see the victim, Amelia Stevens. I'll pop in to see you tomorrow if I get some free time. I've had too many shocks today. I feel as sick as a dog.'

'Say hello to Gwen for me,' said Ted. 'I feel really bad about the old woman, Jack. What's Murray said?'

'He said I'm a suspect and have to be checked out to be eliminated from their enquiries. I was with him yesterday at the crime scene and before that I was eating in the pub. When I got home last night I didn't turn the landing light on, so I didn't notice Stella's door was open.'

'He would say that! He knows you didn't do it, Jack. Don't fret about it. I'll see you tomorrow if you can make it.'

Chapter Seventeen

Lily opened her eyes, she got out of bed and looked at the water in the bowl. She'd slept for more than eight hours. The Doctor hadn't come to punish her. Maybe he was saving it for later. She heard the door open and close. A car door slammed and the engine started. He was going out. Or maybe he was trying to trick her into calling out? She put her ear to the door and listened as the sound of tyres on gravel became faint as the car moved away.

'Catherine! Catherine! Are you okay?'

Catherine's silence worried her. She wondered if the Doctor had killed her.

As she filled the bowl to do her washing, tears ran down her cheeks. Nana, Kitty, Miss Baker and her daddy. She said a silent goodbye to all of them in her mind. If Catherine was dead her only hope was if the Doctor wanted his baby to live. Her stomach ached and she thought of her nana and Kitty and all the lovely cakes and puddings they made in their big old fashioned kitchen at Bumble Cottage. It always smelled of cinnamon, lemon and other mouth-watering aromas.

*

Michael was elated as he drove towards Bordley. He'd searched through some old books and found a few family photographs, one with an address written on the back. He found them when he cleaned out the shed and was burning stuff in the garden. When he'd taken a closer look at the other books, he found more pictures hidden between the pages. The best one was for Goldilocks. It was one of himself when he was about twelve years old, taken in the lounge of the children's home. After a bit of touching up on the computer, he could easily pass it off for a fourteen-year-old.

The information he'd been looking for was there all the time, but he hadn't bothered to look when he'd brought the boxes from his grandmother's house. The authorities must have kept her informed about him right up until her death. Eight years he'd been locked up, before he was allowed to claim what was rightfully his.

He'd suffered long and hard for his inheritance and intended to make people pay for that suffering. He was put in the children's home because his parents had not made any arrangements for him to be looked after in the event of their deaths. They were in their forties and probably hadn't expected death to come so soon. His grandmother had turned her back on him, but her house was now his. He'd been there a few times over the last few months. It was in a bad state of repair and he was clearing it out to sell it.

The manor had been their country home. A large

rambling place, with six bedrooms, four bathrooms, a library, a dining room, three sitting rooms, a huge kitchen, the two rooms at the back of the house where he kept the girls, a double garage, a workshop and other outbuildings. There were also two cars, and a motorcycle his father had used to ride round their property. He'd changed the colour and number plates of his mother's Escort and his father's Audi several times. He was amazed how well preserved they were in the garage. They were purchased just a year before his parents died, so had seen little use when he got back from Dublin. He put new oil and filters in them, air in the tyres and checked that the brakes weren't seized up. Both been covered with dust sheets and the garage, which was added when his father bought the place, was a solid brick building that had been securely locked.

He used the Audi when he took the first girl, Amelia, the one he'd dumped on the nature reserve. It had been easy to get her to go with him. He waved the little bag of white powder and she was in the car like a shot. He knew her habits well from time past.

He rubbed his leg. It had taken years and a lot of pain to get it to how it was now.

It was still painful at times and the scars would be there forever, but it was more or less straight. He strengthened it by running in the fields at the back of the manor. He'd been parked ten minutes outside the neat detached house he was watching. A car came along the road and stopped outside it. A middle-aged couple got out and gathered shopping bags from the boot of the car. The woman was small framed with short grey hair. The man was taller and broader, balding, with a neat grey goatee beard. They were the couple in the photograph.

At last he'd found what he'd been looking for since he'd come back from Dublin.

This family member was going to get the surprise of his life. The thought of their meeting made butterflies dance in his stomach and his bladder threatened to burst.

Chapter Eighteen

As Jack left Ted at the hospital, Gwen O' Brien called from the mortuary to tell him DS Morgan was waiting for him, and she had some unsettling information about Amelia Stevens.

Jack had known Gwen for many years. She was the Chief Forensic Pathologist for the police. Sometimes her testing and re-testing drove people up the wall, but Jack knew there was no-one better at the job. She had fought hard to get where she was, a woman in a man's world, and was highly respected for it.

Jack had been in love with her when they studied law at university. The first things he'd noticed about her were her hypnotic blue eyes, her flowing chestnut hair and the way she blushed when people spoke to her. That blush completely bowled him over. Their romance lasted twelve months when Gwen decided to swap her course and university, and go into forensics and pathology. He hadn't seen her for ten years, when she moved to Dudstone, along with her husband, Jonathon, who was a G.P. and their son, William. Jonathon had died of a heart attack three years ago.

Gwen's life revolved around her work and her son and she shied away from social gatherings as much as she could. Jack always looked forward to seeing her and often wondered what life would have been like if they'd stayed together.

*

Catherine opened her eyes. She'd dreamt of her mother, sitting quietly in the conservatory, as she read one of her Catherine Cookson novels. In the dream everything was calm and peaceful. Now, as she looked round the room, hell had returned. She moved slightly and felt the pain again. The monster had drugged her and pushed something inside her. She could feel an ache deep inside where he'd violated her. She wanted to go to the toilet, she wanted to wash the disgusting thing he'd done from her body, but when she moved an overwhelming feeling of nausea came over her and she vomited.

Lily put her ear to the door. She was sure someone moved round the house. It wasn't the Doctor, he'd gone out in his car an hour earlier.

'Hello!' She shook as she said the word. She wanted to hear Catherine, to know that she was still alive.

'Hello, Lily,' Catherine's voice, subdued and weak, a murmur.

'Catherine. Thank god you're alive! I know he's hurt you, but you have to be strong. He's done the same thing to me many times. I'm so sorry for you.'

'Lily there's blood and vomit all over the bed. What shall I do?'

'You'll have to clean it up. Wash the sheets and your robe. He'll punish you if you don't.'

'I'll try. I found a hole under the sink. I'm slowly making it bigger and getting rid of the grit down the toilet and the sink. I can see daylight and grass and trees. I know when it's day and night. It's light at the moment. I'm terrified he'll find it. I know now that he won't hesitate to kill me. I think he had another girl here besides you and me. He said her warts went septic when he cut them off. I think he killed her, Lily. He's cut a mole off my brow. I hope it doesn't become infected.'

'We must make sure we don't get caught calling to each other. He hasn't cut anything off me, so he must have meant someone else. I used to hear someone crying and moaning. It was so awful. I called out to her but she never answered. If she was alive, she would talk to us, don't you think?'

'Yes, I suppose she would, unless she's too terrified or too weak. He doesn't give me much to eat. I think he keeps us weak so we don't fight back. I get confused.'

'I think he drugs our food too. I know it's hard, but if you don't clean your room he will go berserk. Please try, Catherine!'

'Okay. Lily, I'll try. Have a look under your sink. See if you can make a hole too.'

'I don't think I'll be able to Catherine. I'm pregnant. I'm close to giving birth. Be quiet! I think I just heard his car on the gravel.'

*

Jack swung his old Astra on to the car park of the old Dudstone hospital. It wasn't used as a hospital any longer, since a new one had been built five years previously, but the mortuary, which had been there for over a hundred years was still in use. Jack hated the long dark corridors and poor lighting. It reminded him of the workhouse places from a Dickens novel. The place made him feel as if death was something that had to be hidden and he was walking into the bowels of the earth.

'Sorry to keep you waiting.' Jack opened the door to Examination Room 2 and the unwelcoming smell of decaying flesh and disinfectant stung his nostrils. DS Morgan and Gwen were looking at some x-rays. He walked towards them, took the jar of Vapour Rub DS Morgan offered and smeared some under his nose.

'I have some bad news for you. Miss Baker has been attacked and as far as I can see, the attacker left her for dead. She was conscious when I found her but there's not much hope at the moment.'

Gwen went to him and kissed his cheek. 'I'm so sorry, Jack. The poor woman.'

The usual flush appeared on her cheeks and spread to her neck.

Jack felt his own cheeks burn at Gwen's show of affection. 'She's at Dudstone General. I'm going there later. So tell me. What have you found?'

'It appears Amelia Stevens has given birth.' Gwen went on. 'I'm not sure when exactly but I believe it was during the last year.'

'She's been missing for over three years,' said Jack.

He noticed Gwen's hair was lighter and she'd lost a bit of weight.

'I know. DS Morgan has filled me in on the details.'

Jack glanced at DS Morgan, their eyes met briefly and he felt a ripple of nervousness in his stomach, which surprised him.

'If you look at this x-ray of the victim's pelvic bone you can clearly see it's oval in shape. In a woman who hasn't given birth it would be round. There are other indications usually, but the body is so badly decayed I'll have to do more tests.'

'Can you say what caused her death?'

'Not officially, but I've examined what's left of her stomach. I think she was starved and beaten, but I can't rule out infection. She's got a skull fracture. My initial thoughts on that is she was hit with a blunt object. Something like a hammer.'

Jack put a hand through his hair and blew his breath out. 'Phew! Sounds like a right sadistic bastard!' He felt sick. 'He keeps a girl for three years, makes her pregnant, delivers her baby, then violently kills her.'

'Not exactly,' said Gwen. She noticed the colour had drained from Jack's face and pulled her gloved hand from the chest cavity of the body and covered it with a sheet. 'She died from various things. I don't think the hammer blow killed her outright. I think he injured her in many different ways. I've taken samples and swabs from all over her body. I'll get them done as soon as I can.' She peeled her gloves off and threw them in the bin.

'Okay. He caused her death.' Jack moved closer to look at what was left of the girl's face. He had to hold back the retch in his guts. He wondered if Lily had shared the same fate as the poor girl on the slab and looked away.

'He caused her death. Yes, I think we can definitely say that,' said Gwen.

'Brace yourself. You must see this.' She lifted the sheet from the dead girl's feet.

'Oh my god!' Jack moved back startled.

'I suspect rats from the small teeth marks on her ankle bone but I'm not a hundred per cent sure yet. I also found this.' She pointed to a plastic bag with a piece of paper inside. 'I haven't touched it. It was inside her vagina. I removed it with tweezers. I saw it when I examined her feet.'

Jack pulled a pair of latex gloves from his coat pocket and put them on. He took the plastic bag and held it flat on the table to read the note. 'It is better to live in a corner of a house ship than in a house with a quarrelsome wife.'

'What does it mean?' Gwen asked.

'I think it's a biblical quote,' said Jack. 'It implies that Amelia gave him a hard time by quarrelling with him.'

'Her mother said she was outspoken,' said DS Morgan.

'Is there anything else, Gwen?'

'I'd like to know what happened to the baby. There's a strong possibility it died, but if it lived, where is it?'

'We don't know the answer to that yet. Send me your report when you've finished. I know it will be done with your usual attention to detail.' Jack went to go to the door then turned back. 'Oh, Ted sends his love. He's in hospital at the moment waiting for some test results on his sore.'

'Yes, I heard he was ill. Tell him I'll pop down to see him soon.'

'Okay, will do.' Jack looked to DS Morgan and held the door as they went out.

'Come on, we have to get in touch with East Yorkshire. Perhaps they'll send your friend here to deal with it.'

'I doubt it, he's retiring in a few weeks, he's seventy-three.'

Jack looked back and called to Gwen. 'Hair looks nice, by the way.'

Gwen smiled and blushed again.

'Do you fancy a drink later?' said Jack.

'William's coming home from uni. Sorry can't make it tonight, Jack.'

'Maybe another night then. I'll give you a call.' He closed the door. It was the third time Gwen had refused a drink with him and he felt a little embarrassed for asking her out again.

As they walked along the dark corridor DS Morgan wiped the Vapour Rub from under her nose with a tissue, then offered one to Jack.

'I'll see you back at the station then?' he said as he took the tissue.

131

'Could you give me a lift, sir? I got Constable Hadley to bring me here, my car's off the road.'

Jack gave her a look, wiped his nose and gave the used tissue back to her. 'I'm not a bloody taxi service, you know.'

'Thanks!' She took the tissue with her fingertips and dropped it in an evidence bag.

Jack looked bemused. 'You have my DNA on that. Are you planning to frame me for something?'

'Sounds like a plan.' She didn't smile.

They walked across the car park to Jack's car and he clicked it open. 'Okay, get in then, Ginger, if you can find a space in the rubble.'

DS Morgan opened the door to find the front seat littered with clothes and food containers. 'Don't call me Ginger! The last person who did that lost two teeth. I'll move these to the back seat then?'

'Yes, yes, anywhere. Throw them in the street if you want to. There's no need to threaten violence.'

'What's that smell?'

'I can't smell anything,' said Jack.

'There must be something wrong with your nose. Are you sure you haven't got a dead body in the boot?' DS Morgan fidgeted and pulled a small hammer from under her backside.

'Well, I might have, I haven't opened it lately. Do you want to go and check?'

'No thanks. I'll hold my breath.'

'That might be a good idea.' Jack smiled, clicked

on the cassette player and began to sing along with Frankie Valli and the Four Seasons' 'Bye-Bye Baby', well aware of the daggers that stabbed the side of his face.

'What the hell do you use this for?' DS Morgan held up the hammer.

'Well, this car is temperamental, like all females. I have to give her engine a clout with it now and again to make her realise who's boss. So you'd better be careful.'

'For god's sake! Are you for real? You know, you remind me of someone.'

Jack turned the music down. 'Who?'

'I'm not sure yet but it will come to me.'

'Well make sure he's good looking when you think of him. I'm known to bear grudges. So don't piss me off.' He cut her a look and revved the engine.

'Oh! Things not going well with Professor O'Brien?'

'Mind your own business! There's nothing there that needs to go well!'

'Sorry! Obviously a sore subject. I won't mention her again.'

'Keep that in mind and we'll get on fine,' said Jack.

Jack dropped DS Morgan back at the station and popped to his flat to check on Polly. He'd moved the cat to his flat while Miss Baker was in hospital. He put some food and fresh water in the kitchen and was about the go out when something shiny caught his eye. As he bent down by the door to pick it up he realised it was a ring. He turned it round in his fingers. Lily's ring. Had the bastard who attacked Stella left it there for him? Or had it been there all the time?

*

As he walked along the hospital corridor Jack thought he was going to faint and had to stop and lean on the wall for a few seconds. He hadn't had anything to eat since breakfast and he'd spent all day visiting hospitals and the morgue. He felt drained.

Constable Hadley had been assigned to sit outside Miss Baker's room to vet all visitors and stood up when he saw Jack.

'Any news on her condition, Hadley?'

'She's still unconscious, sir. The doctor said she was mumbling a bit before they operated but he couldn't understand what she was saying. There's a doctor in with her now.'

'Oh, Hadley I forgot to ask you about your relationship with Catherine Bennett.'

Hadley blushed. 'We're just friends, sir. We go around with the same people.'

'That's all?' Jack gave him a long look as he opened the door to Miss Baker's room.

'Yes sir, that's all.'

The doctor turned round to look at Jack as he went in.

'I'm Inspector Riley,' said Jack. 'Can you tell me how she's doing?'

'I'm Doctor Bird. I'll be looking after Miss Baker

while she's here. All I can tell you at the moment is she's breathing on her own now.' He was a man in his sixties, with bushy grey hair and a wrinkled brow. 'The cuts weren't as deep as they looked in the first instance. She was cut with a razor blade or a scalpel. I'd say a scalpel. I'm stunned she survived to be honest. She's a strong woman.'

'She'll recover then?'

'I'm not going to forecast that, Inspector. It's a class three haemorrhage, which is a thirty to forty per cent loss of her total blood. She's had a transfusion. She's also had a six-hour operation to repair the damage to her body. The cuts were done downwards in the shape of a large 'x' but they weren't deep and they missed every major artery. You never can tell what the shock might do to her. We'll see what the next forty-eight hours bring.'

'Do you think that the person who did this could be a doctor?'

'I would think they have some medical knowledge. It wasn't a frenzied attack. It was slow and deliberate. Extremely painful for the poor woman.'

*

At Bordley General Hospital Ted Bateman was having his brow examined by consultant, Mr Douglas Darby, a fat, balding man who must have been near retirement age, and a tall young man with neatly combed dark hair, a short beard and black rimmed spectacles.

'I hope you don't mind my junior, Doctor Munroe, being present Mr Batman, only I like my staff to see as many types of skin diseases as they can. All good experience for the future.'

'I don't mind at all,' said Bateman as he looked the young man over. 'How long do you think I'll be in here, Doc? Oh, and I'm not Batman, I'm Bateman. I haven't got a cape, just an old raincoat,' Ted chuckled.

Mr Darby cringed. 'I'm not sure yet, but I will release you as soon as possible, Mr Bateman. I'm sure you don't like being confined like a prisoner, if you'll excuse the pun. Oh, and I'm not doc, I'm Mr Darby please. We have certain standards of etiquette here.'

'Of course D… Mr Darby.'

'Come closer, Munroe. I want you to look at the edges of this growth to see if there are similarities to the last one we looked at. I must say it's a rather vicious looking thing. He's probably infected it with dirty fingernails. What do you think?'

Ted grimaced and inspected his fingernails.

'It does look a little inflamed, Mr Darby. Could it be a pre-cancerous growth, sir?'

Munroe offered. 'Actinic keratosis.'

'Nail on the head! Well done, Munroe! I'll get some pictures taken. We can use this as a case study for the students. For god's sake don't let anyone touch it without gloved hands. We don't know what's lurking in those scabs.'

Ted opened his book as they left the room. The young doctor reminded him of someone, but he couldn't for the life of him think who it was. Within a few minutes he was back in his book, trying to figure out who the second kidnapper was in James Patterson's *Along Came a Spider*.

Chapter Nineteen

Doctor Steven Munroe finished his shift at Conley Hospital at 8pm. As he drove home he thought about the sleepless night he'd had and the raging headache that had followed it. Another round of nightmares and dark images of the person whose face he couldn't see, pulling him, holding him so close to the fire. As the person turned to face him the dream ended.

He was going to speak to his parents about his other family tonight. His birth parents had died, but he never asked how or where. His adoptive parents never spoke of them and he felt it was a betrayal to them to search for his past as if he wasn't grateful to them, but he was sure the haunting dreams were in some way connected to what had happened to his real parents.

The Munroes had told him that shortly after they'd agreed to adopt him he'd fallen from his bedroom window at the children's home while trying to retrieve a homemade kite that had snagged on a tree branch. He'd been in a coma for two weeks and when he woke up had no memory of his past. Three months later he went to live with the Munroes.

Nightmares had plagued his teenage years. He woke up in sweats, he wet the bed, sometimes he called out. They finally left him when he went to medical school. Now they were back, more disturbing than ever.

When he got in, his parents were in the kitchen making supper, his mother filled the teapot with boiling water, his father made cheese on toast.

'You want some, Stevie?' his father asked as bread jumped from the toaster.

'Yes please. Do you have some painkillers, mom? My head's bouncing.'

His mother went to him and felt his brow. 'You're working too hard, Stevie. Too many long hours.' She moved to the cupboard to search for tablets.

'They'll not thank you for knocking yourself up, lad. Take a few days off why don't you?' His father put a plate in front of him.

'Most of the other junior doctors are having it hard too. We work twelve, fourteen-hour shifts and get no overtime. It's the same at all the other hospitals all over the country. I've heard talk of strikes, but I can't agree with it. I'm off now for ten days.' He took a bite of toast. 'I was thinking of doing a bit of research while I'm away camping.'

'What kind of research, lad? To do with your work?'

'Well, I was thinking more of family history.' He studied the food he was eating to avoid eye contact with his father.

'The birth records of my parents and grandparents are upstairs in a folder, and your mother's. Isn't that right Gaynor?'

His mother placed two painkillers next to his plate. 'Yes, dear.'

'Well, I was thinking more of my other family.'

His mother put her hand to her mouth. 'Whatever for?'

'We're your family, Stevie. What do you want to go looking up the past for? Can't you see it will upset your mother?'

His mother's startled reaction shocked him. He wondered what kind of secret could make the colour drain from her face. What kind of family did he once belong to?

'I don't wish to upset anyone. And I'm not going to look for relatives. I just want to know where I come from, that's all. Is that too much to ask?'

'Why, lad? What good will it do you to know?'

'I think there's something in my past that keeps giving me these nightmares.' He picked up the tablets and swallowed them with a gulp of tea. 'I'm having trouble sleeping, you see. It's always the same dream. There's a fire and someone's holding me back and I can't see his face. I want to know who he is.'

He noticed the black look that passed between his parents. His mother stumbled as she came to sit at the table. His father jumped up and went to her.

'See how you've upset your mother now? We don't want to know about the past. You shouldn't either. This is your family and we don't want to hear any more of this nonsense. You're having dreams because you're working too hard, that's all.'

'Anyone would think they were serial killers the way you react. I don't think it's unreasonable for me to want to know where I came from. I'm sorry if it upsets you so much, I won't mention it to either of you again. Just forget I asked.'

Chapter Twenty

Catherine managed to do her washing and clean herself up before the Doctor came with her food. He watched her through the peephole as she sat on the bed. 'The Funeral March of a Marionette' played in the background. The bolts slid across, one, two, three.

'Well, well, Catherine. You have done yourself proud today! Perhaps I'll reward you with an extra biscuit later. I do hope you've learned your lesson. I have to decide what to do with you now. You're soiled. Soiled goods are imperfect. I was going to be gentle with you, Catherine, and let you fall in love with me in your own time. But it now seems I don't have to bother with those preliminaries. After all, I can take what I want now. You are mine to do as I please. It's your fault if I bring someone else here. You've pushed me, Catherine. I already have my eye on someone. She's a little angel.' He placed the tray of food on the bed. 'Now eat your food. Think yourself lucky that I'm in a good mood today. Oh, did I tell you? I've found someone I've been looking for. What a wonderful surprise it will be for him.' He poked a spidery finger in her chest and spun round like a dancer. 'Be quiet, be careful and be good. You, my dear, are living on borrowed time. Who took your Virginity, Catherine? Was it that young policeman I saw you with? Or was it your father? You talk about him in your sleep, you know. I don't think Hadley had it in him somehow.'

Catherine shook and looked away from his eyes. Tears ran down her cheeks.

'I was right!' He shouted and pointed a finger in her face. 'It was your dirty father, wasn't it? Did you like him fucking you?' He leaned across the bed, grabbed her arm and dug his nails in to her flesh. 'You're nothing but a slut! You hear me! A dirty fucking slut! The nakedness of thy father, or the nakedness of thy mother, thou shalt not uncover!' He let go of her arm and slapped her across the face with the back of his hand. 'I'll be back later to finish this.'

Catherine washed blood from her arm. She noticed he hadn't limped when he came into the room, nor when he left. The hole under the sink was getting bigger. The three large stones she'd dislodged were balanced on the ones she was working on. He hadn't inspected things closely for a day or two. Perhaps he was confident there was no escape for her. Perhaps there wasn't, but she had to try, or die trying. She bent down to look under the sink and moved the bucket. When she strained her ears, she could hear birds singing. It made her think of home, her garden, her mother, her father.

He was right about her father. She sat on the floor and thought about the first time her father had touched her. She was eight years old. Her mother was having one of her breakdowns at the time. It hadn't happened for over a year now and she was determined it would never happen again. She'd learned how to avoid being alone with her father. She wouldn't give in to his cruel form of blackmail anymore, but it hung over her like a huge black cloud. Throughout her school years she imagined that everyone who looked at her knew what she'd been doing. Even her closest friends, Leanne and Alice. She'd come so close to telling them many times but always backed out. The thought of losing them was too much to bear. She put the bucket back, closed the cupboard and went to her bed.

A door closed and she heard a car start up. The Doctor had gone out. Then she heard Lily.

'Beautiful dreamer wake unto me…'

'Lily!'

'Catherine! Are you okay?'

'Yes, I'm okay! He's going to get another girl, Lily. He told me. It's because of me! He knows a friend of mine too. He said his name.'

'No, Catherine! It's not because of you. It's because he's a maniac and a vile abuser! Who is your friend?'

'His name's Andy. He's a police constable. Do you think the Doctor might be someone I know Lily? I thought I'd heard his voice before.'

'It sounds like it. If Andy is a policeman he probably knows my father.'

'Do you think we'll ever get away from here? I've found the hole and I'm trying to make it bigger but I think he's going to kill me before I can do it.'

'Don't say that! Don't say or do anything to upset him! We can't let him catch us talking again! What if the Doctor is a policeman? He's going to know about everything they're doing to find us. He's always going to be one step ahead of them.'

'I hope not. If he is we'll never leave here. I'm going to work on the hole. I have to get out, Lily, before it's too late! Don't worry, I'll send someone back for you! He hasn't got a limp at all. And he doesn't feel he has to pretend anymore because he knows I'm not leaving here.'

'We must fight till the end, Catherine. Don't give up. I'm still here after all this time. We have to hope that one day we'll go back to our happy lives with the people we love.'

'My life wasn't really happy, Lily. I have a terrible secret.'

'I don't know you, but I can tell you're not a bad person. Don't judge yourself. Nothing is that bad that it can't be sorted out. Think of the situation we're in now. Can anything ever be this bad?'

'I suppose not. But it is something so terrible you would hate me.'

'You don't have to tell me if you don't want to. I won't hate you, Catherine. I can't hate people who have done me no harm.'

'I've never told anyone. I don't know what to do about it.'

'You poor girl. You can tell me anything, Catherine. I won't judge you.'

'I can't, Lily. You sound such a nice person. I can't wait to see you. What do you look like?'

'I have blond hair and blue eyes. What about you?'

'The same. Perhaps the Doctor chose us for that reason.'

'He talks about angels a lot. He's a religious maniac.'

'Sometimes he calls me Rebecca and he puts his head in my lap and tells me to stroke it.'

'He said and did those things to me when I first came here. Now he calls me a slut. I think my time has almost run out, Catherine.'

Chapter Twenty-One

It was after nine when Jack pulled up outside Bumble Cottage. Kitty's old blue Morris Traveller was parked on the drive. His mother and Kitty were in the kitchen cutting up vegetables.

'Two visits this week,' his mother said as he closed the door. 'We are honoured.'

'When did you last see Fisheye?' Jack asked as he pulled out a chair and sat down at the table. His eyes rested on a painting of his great, great grandfather, Thomas O' Riley, and he wondered why his mother had put it on the kitchen wall.

'Fisheye?' His mother carried on chopping.

'Don't sound so bloody surprised, Mother! I know he's been here.'

'My visitors are none of your business.'

'He's brought a load of stolen DVD players and TVs from Dover and you asked me to try to sell them.'

'I haven't seen him.'

'You're a bloody liar, Mother! I could nick you right now!'

'Go on then.'

'Thieving's in your genes.'

'The same genes you have,' his mother retorted.

'Why do you keep doing this? You're loaded with the spoils of years of smuggling from your bloody great grandfather! You don't need the money.'

His mother put her knife down and turned to look at him. 'But I need the excitement, Jack!' She said with a twinkle in her eye.

Kitty laughed out loud, put her knife down and went to fill the kettle. 'Oh, Rosie! You are a devil! You want a cup of tea, Jack? Or a whiskey?'

Jack put his head in his hands and sighed loudly. 'You don't get it, do you? The pair of you think it's just a game! I'm surprised at you, Kitty! I didn't think you of all people would encourage her. Where was his next drop?'

'Don't give him whiskey, Kitty, he's a drunk.' His mother wiped her hands on her apron and put three cups on a tray. 'Would you like a slice of egg custard with your tea, Jack?'

'You're not going to tell me, are you? I don't want you to sell anymore and I don't want you locked up. I'm going to have a word with Fisheye. Can't you just behave like normal old women?'

'We are not old!' his mother shouted. 'We're in our prime. Now shut up and eat your tart!'

'I'm going to forget I've seen the stolen goods

here,' said Jack as he picked up a spoon to eat the tart. 'I don't want to see any more. You hear me?'

'Yes, we hear you,' said his mother as she put some tart in her mouth. 'Oh, isn't this delicious?'

'Another four grams of saturated fat,' Jack sighed. 'And I'm sitting in a den of thieves.'

'Shut up!' his mother snapped. 'You sound like an old man!'

Chapter Twenty-Two

Tuesday morning

Jack hadn't slept much. He was in a turmoil about what to do about the ring. Should he share its discovery with Murray, or keep it to himself? If he told Murray there would be a definite connection between Miss Baker's assault and Lily's disappearance. Cases he couldn't work on. He was convinced the crimes had been committed by the same man and working on Catherine Bennett's abduction would lead him to Lily. He decided to keep the find to himself for the time being and headed for work. He was also fighting a battle in his mind with his mother and his conscience.

When he got to the station he checked to see if there were any new developments in the Bennett case, then read a fax which had been left on his desk. It was a list of the stolen electrical goods from Dover. Two hundred DVD players and a hundred flat screen TVs. He sighed. Murray had written on the bottom: *Make everyone aware of this, Jack*. He folded the fax and put it in his pocket.

The market was busy today. Jack wove his way through the crowds, past the vegetable stall, then the old lady who sold wool and sewing accessories. She'd been there even before Jack had moved to the town. She sat in her folding chair knitting squares for refugee blankets, occasionally glancing up to smile at potential customers.

Joey Coombs was giving out his usual spiel to a crowd that had gathered round him. 'Come on, who wants to buy one? Only a tenner. Top quality.' He noticed Jack in the crowd and went quiet.

'I'd like a word with you, Joey,' said Jack.

The crowd dispersed and Joey turned to him. 'You're bad for business, Inspector.'

'Where did you get those DVD players, Joey?'

'None o' ya business.'

'It is if they're stolen.'

'I bought 'em.'

'Where from? Have you got a receipt?'

'Why do ya want to know?'

'Because I think they're stolen. Now, who sold them to you?'

'Father Christmas.'

'Joey, I happen to know that they were stolen in Dover. Now do you want to go down for receiving stolen goods?'

'I didn't steal nothing. I bought 'em off an old bloke with a glass eye. He said they were old stock from a warehouse that was closing down.'

'An old bloke with a glass eye? What type of vehicle did he drive?'

'It was a white van. But he wasn't there. It was another bloke who delivered them. I met him on the car park of Toys-R-Us.'

'How did you get in touch with him?'

'The old bloke with the glass eye came here to ask if I wanted to buy them and told me where to go. I think he was Irish. He spoke a bit funny like. He weren't from round here.'

Jack suppressed a smile. Either Fisheye was trying to disguise his southern accent or Joey hadn't a clue about accents.

'How many did you buy?'

'Fifty. I already sold ten.'

'Pack them up. I'll send someone round to collect them.'

'What about the two hundred and fifty quid I paid for 'em?'

'If you've sold ten, you've only lost a hundred and fifty quid. Your loss. I've told you before about buying stolen goods. Pack them up.'

'Mr Riley, I got four kids and the missis is up the duff again with twins. I cor stand the loss.'

'Well you should make sure your dealings are honest, Joey. My hands are tied now. I have to report where I found them. You weren't bothered about your family when you were arguing over that woman the other night.'

'I was telling him not to go with her, Mr Riley.

She's got the clap. He thought I wanted her for meself, but I wouldn't touch her with a bargepole. I hate women like that. I got a good un Mr Riley. I wouldn't do anythink across 'er.' Jack gave him a long look. 'I'll see what I can do. But I can't promise anything.'

*

Back at the station Jack found Wallace and told him to go round to the market and pick up the stolen goods. He was right. Fisheye was at it again. He would call him later.

When Jack arrived at the hospital, Doctor Bird and a female nurse were in Miss Baker's room. The nurse checked a drip that was attached to the old woman's arm.

'Inspector! Good news! Miss Baker is showing signs of recovery. We have her in an induced coma at the moment but her vital signs are good. We plan to bring her round tomorrow morning if you'd like to be present. We have given her body a rest to begin the healing process.' The doctor was looking at Miss Baker's chart. 'She's breathing on her own, her heartbeat and blood pressure are normal.'

'That is good news,' said Jack. 'What time shall I come tomorrow?'

'Make it about ten.'

*

'Look, it's not a mathematical equation! I only asked if you wanted to go get some lunch! It's fine by me if you don't want to.' Jack turned from DS Morgan and dropped a folder on his desk. 'I'll be in the pub if you need me. If the chief asks, I'm on a case.'

'That's dishonest!' The red flames bounced as she turned her head.

'Are you my conscience, or what? I am entitled to eat you know. Plus, the boss is always doing it. You look like you could do with a good meal yourself. Why are you waiting in my office anyway?'

'Professor O'Brien said she might fax some stuff over about Amelia. And I haven't been allocated an office yet.'

Jack turned to her and smiled. 'I know just the place for you DS Morgan. Follow me.' He opened the door and went into the corridor. 'It's just along here.' He turned right, stopped outside a room and opened the door. 'There you go.'

'That's not funny, Inspector.' The storage room was full of boxes and old chairs.

'Well are you coming for lunch or not? The fax will be here when we get back. It will probably have my name on it anyway.'

DS Morgan hesitated. 'Oh, okay. I'll come and get something, but I'm not drinking alcohol.'

'Please yourself. Don't you think you'd be more suited to another job?'

'Like what?'

'A nun, perhaps.'

'Sarcasm doesn't become you, Inspector.' She flicked hair from her shoulder with the back of her hand. 'I would have thought you could come up with something better than a cliché. And when am I going to get my own office?'

'I'll try harder next time,' said Jack. 'There might be an empty cupboard on the first floor that you can squeeze into for the time being.'

The Bull and Bear was quiet and Jack steered DS Morgan to a table near the window. 'I like to see who's coming and going. Make sure none of the bastards I've locked up come behind me,' he said as they sat down.

'Haven't you considered that they could shoot you through this window and make a clean getaway?'

'No, I haven't, Clever Clogs,' said Jack. 'What would you like to eat?'

'Well, I don't know really.'

'Shall I surprise you?'

'I feel I'm taking a risk here, but go on then. I'll have an orange juice as well.'

Jack went to the bar, ordered the food, shared a joke with Mat the licensee and said hello to a few colleagues who'd just finished their shift.

'Now what can you remember from the Amelia Stevens case?' He put the drinks on the table and sat next to DS Morgan.

'Well, I remember thinking the taxi drivers hadn't been questioned about any taxis that shouldn't have been on their patch. The DI in charge didn't have his heart in the case. When he found out she was a drug addict it's like he thought she wasn't worth bothering with. He was retired twelve months later.'

'You didn't question?'

'No. I was new, wasn't I? Who was going to listen to me? They didn't like me.'

Jack smiled and opened his mouth to speak…

'And before your mind starts working overtime, it was because I came from somewhere else. I wasn't one of them. My uncle was the Chief Constable. They thought he pulled strings to get me there.'

'Did he?'

'No! I worked bloody hard!'

'Handy though. You know, to tell people that.'

'I never told anyone. It was a D.C. who found out and told everyone. To be honest I was glad to be sent here. I was fed up with the insinuations.'

The food arrived.

'Oh my god! What are they?'

'It's faggots an pays,' said Jack and smiled.

'What?'

'Faggots and peas. Don't ask questions. Just try them.'

'It looks disgusting.'

'Eat it, woman! You'll be surprised.' Jack shovelled a mouthful down.

They ate in silence for a few minutes.

'Well? What do you think? said Jack.

'Okay, but I'm not that impressed. What meat is it?'

'You don't have to bother with such minor details. It's the taste that matters.'

DS Morgan stopped eating. 'What are they made from?'

'Offal,' said Jack.

'What?'

'Liver, kidney, brains, caul…'

'That's enough… I'm not eating them again… ever!'

'They'll grow on you.'

'Well they actually look like something that might grow on you.'

'Balls, you mean?'

'Yes.'

Jack laughed out loud.

*

He was only a few feet away from them. He couldn't hear what they were saying, but they seemed to be having a good time. DS Morgan was very attractive, obviously not pure from the way she flashed her eyes at Jack Riley. He wondered how long it would take Riley to get her into bed.

*

'I think it's a good idea to look at CCTV again,' said Jack. 'Perhaps we can try to find what make of car was used. We could look at CCTV around the town and on the car parks.'

'I can try to trace the witness who said she saw Amelia get in it, sir.'

He leaned towards her and whispered. 'You can call me Jack when we're in the pub, you know, lighten up a bit.' He smiled. 'You've got gravy on your nose.'

'Oh.' She blushed and wiped her nose with a serviette.

Jack finished his pint and put the glass down. 'So, shall we go back and see what Gwen has sent us?'

'Yes. Is it right the station is haunted by the ghost of someone who hanged himself there?'

'I believe that's the general consensus, though I have to admit I've never seen it. Jackie Smith, a chimney sweep. I think it was eighteen-ninety. He was found guilty of raping and murdering a doctor's maid. The doctor confessed to the crime on his death bed.'

'Thank god for forensics,' said DS Morgan.

*

He was sat chatting with a group of firemen when Jack Riley waved to them as he left the Bull and Bear with the pretty DS. After all, he was invisible, he was probably one of the last people Riley would suspect.

*

The fax was waiting when they got back. Jack tore it from the machine. 'She died from a fractured skull, malnutrition and septicaemia. My god! There is also evidence she had an operation on her right leg. Gwen thinks it was about seven years ago, and it was to lengthen the bone. She had several small scars on her left arm and her back. Possibly from having something like cysts or warts removed. Some of them were quite recent. The teeth marks on her feet bones were made by rats. There's another fax from forensics. There was a hair and skin tissue found on the plastic sheeting Amelia's body was wrapped in. They're with the lab team now. The plastic sheet was the kind you could buy in any hardware store but there were wood fibres stuck to it that were not from the area where the body was found. It's possible they were from some kind of shed flooring.'

There was a knock on the door and Murray came in. 'Have you seen the papers, Jack?'

'No, sir.'

'Someone has tipped them off about you being a suspect in the attack on Miss Baker. He calls himself 'Hot Source'. I'll have to call a press conference for tomorrow to say you've been eliminated from the enquiries. Have you spoken to anyone about it?'

'No, sir.' He lied, he wasn't going to mention Ted.

'Well someone has. I hope it's no-one on the team.'

'Why would anyone want to implicate me in the attack on Miss Baker?'

'I don't know. Maybe they're just assuming because you live there. You're not allowed to investigate it anyway because of your relationship with her. Everyone on the team would know that. Have you made any enquiries about the stolen electrical goods yet?'

'I have it covered, sir. I've recovered some from the local market which were bought in good faith. I'm pretty sure the stallholder didn't steal them or know they were stolen. I don't think there's any need to charge him with anything.'

'Jack, these market traders know something's stolen when they're offered cheap goods. Are you going soft?'

'Not at all, sir.'

'Receiving stolen goods! Charge him!'

'Yes, sir. I'll pass it to DS Jones if that's okay with you, sir. I'm up to my neck with the Bennett case. The samples from the plastic sheet Amelia was wrapped in are still being examined. Do we have to assume we're dealing with two separate crimes? A kidnapping and a murder committed by two different people?'

'We do at the moment. I need to allocate a team for the Castle banquet tomorrow night. Superintendent Middleton thinks it's an ideal place for a terrorist attack.'

'The what?'

'The medieval banquet at Dudstone Castle. The Mayor, Mayoress and other local dignitaries will be attending. We're expecting a large crowd. Dudstone Little Theatre are performing *The Taming of the Shrew* in the castle grounds. The Mayor has invited me and Superintendent Middleton.'

Before he went home Jack went to find DS Jones to tell him about the stolen goods and Joey Coombs. Jones had already gone home. Jack wrote him a note and put it on his desk with the case folder. He was about to leave but looked back at the note and folder. There were two or three other folders on the desk and he picked them up and put his note and folder inside one of them.

It was after seven when Jack got home that evening. He moved some books and papers from the settee and sat down to call Fisheye. He answered after a couple of rings.

'Hello, Jackie, me lad. How you doing?'

'Don't Jackie me! You've been to my mother's house with some stolen goods again. I've told you before not to bring stuff on my patch.'

'It's a one-off Jackie. I just gave them to Rosie as a present like, not to sell. Won't happen again.'

'You said that last time.'

'I got kind of lumbered with them. They're all gone now though.'

'They'd better be. I've had to put an idiot on the case. This doesn't lead to my mother's door, Fisheye. You hear me?'

'The rest might be up in Manchester,' said Fisheye. 'That's all I'm saying.'

'Are they round the markets?'

'Thieves honour, Jack! I got to go now, got a domino game waiting at the Fisherman's. I'll see thee lad.'

Chapter Twenty-Three

Wednesday

Jack and DS Morgan were watching CCTV footage of the night Amelia Stevens had gone missing.

'East Yorkshire say the girl was found in our jurisdiction, so we have to deal with it and keep them informed. They'll help as much as they can but can't spare anyone to come down at the moment. I'm not that good with computers,' Jack admitted. 'There's a laptop at home that Lily used to talk to her friends on social media. They took it away when she went missing, examined it, but nothing was found that could give a clue as to where she was.'

'You must miss her terribly.'

'Yes,' said Jack. He swallowed to get rid of the lump in his throat. 'You know the area on here pretty well, don't you? Let's see if we can find anything that was missed before.'

'There were lots of cameras in the town centre.' DS Morgan sat down next to him. 'You see that car park to the right of the picture? It's pretty close to the club Amelia visited with her friends. There's another camera on the other side of it. The footage from that will follow.'

'Can we get a look at some of the registration numbers?'

DS Morgan took the mouse. 'We can try, if I zoom in.'

'I'm looking for this one. A witness took it on the day Catherine Bennett went missing and Wallace found it on a camera driving out of town. Claude Benson owns it now. Murray said he bought the car about fifteen years ago. It was an old Ford Anglia in pristine condition. He bought new number plates a couple of years back. Obviously everyone who works for him will be interviewed and possibly DNA tested. Murray's arranged for me to question him later.'

DS Morgan looked at the car registration number. 'Let's see. We have to consider that East Yorkshire didn't have a number to go on. If they had, things would have been a lot different. He wouldn't have used it to take Catherine. He might not have used it to take Amelia.'

'I know but we have to look at all possibilities. I'm not criticising anyone's work. I want to find out what happened to Amelia. Can we just check the two car parks closest to the club please?'

'Okay.'

'Gwen said Amelia had had an operation on her left leg to lengthen the bone. That would mean she once had a limp wouldn't it?'

DS Morgan turned to look at him. 'Yes, and the

young woman from the library said the man she saw had a limp. Do you think there's some connection with Amelia and the man from the library? Perhaps they had operations at the same hospital.'

'Now you're thinking like me. We believe that the abductor has dark hair because of the DNA on the handkerchief. The man seen at the library was fair haired.'

'If he was picking out his next victim, Catherine, don't you think he would wear a disguise? He knows he's going to be seen if he's going there to watch her.'

'That's what Ted Bateman said. It could explain why Amelia got in the car. She might have known him. I think we'd better do some checks. Get in touch with Amelia's parents and find out where and when she had her operations. I'm going to concentrate on the car. Then I want to have a look at the library CCTV for the last month. Catherine's abductor might be on there in the weeks preceding her disappearance. Murray's holding a press conference at this minute to say I'm not a suspect in the in the attack on Miss Baker. He's releasing CCTV footage from outside the tailor's, showing a man wearing a baseball cap and blue overalls entering the flats on Sunday when I was with him at the crime scene.'

'Have you any idea who might try to implicate you?'

'I think it's the person who attacked Stella. Whether he's on the team or not, I don't know. I certainly hope not. What kind of person are we looking for in connection with the kidnappings?'

'A very disturbed one. I think it's probably

something from his childhood. Perhaps his parents were strict. They might have abused him. People who do these kind of things are sometimes bullied at home or school. They are inadequate but get the feeling of power from taking someone or killing them. If he's also got a crippled leg, he could have been ridiculed for it. I'd say he's single and a loner. But it's not always the case. Sometimes seemingly happily married men commit these crimes. Look at the Boston Strangler, hc had a wife and daughter. Our man has to have somewhere to take his victims. That's why I think he's not married. It has to be out of the way, in case they make a noise or scream. Unless he's soundproofed his house. If he's got a job he will not mix with the other workers and he might only do part time work. He'll want to spend time with his victims. Of course some kidnappers can't be put in to any kind of mould. '

'Why would he keep them alive? Have babies with them?'

'For him there has to be a point to it all. Something from his childhood could have triggered it. He could be trying to prove something or be accepted. Or just have control over someone. To have the power over someone's life.'

'Okay. He has control when he's got them, so why does he let them die, Sandy?'

'Because he can. He obviously thinks he doesn't need them anymore, so he gets another one. He has no conscience or empathy. He doesn't think that what he does is wrong. He takes them, he operates on them. I'd say he's trying to make them look better. He obviously has some medical knowledge. Perhaps he failed his exams at medical school. That's another area we could look in if we have no luck with the leg connection.'

'He's taken Catherine. If he's got Lily's her time is running out.'

'I don't like to say it, but yes, he might be getting desperate, especially now he knows the car registration was clocked.'

'We'll have a couple of hours on here, then I'll go to the hospital to see Miss Baker.'

'How is she?'

'Well, she's responding to treatment. Just about holding her own.'

'Are you going to the play at the castle?' DS Morgan pulled something out of a plastic carrier bag. She lifted it up to show Jack. 'I got this from the local market on my way in yesterday morning. A tenner. Can you believe it?' She held up a DVD player, identical to the one his mother had shown him.

'If I were you I wouldn't let the chief see that. I'll say two words. Stolen goods. I've got about forty in the store confiscated from the market. Didn't you hear the chief asking me about them yesterday? Just go and put it with them, or keep it well hidden.' Jack smiled. 'I won't tell anyone you've been buying stolen goods and no I'm not going to the play. I'll be collecting DNA samples from the blokes at the scrap yard.'

'Oh my god! The stolen electrical goods!' DS Morgan sighed and dropped the DVD player back in the bag as if it had suddenly burst into flames.

*

Jack arrived at the hospital fifteen minutes late. Miss Baker was sitting up in bed drinking tea through a straw from a plastic cup. All the tubes had been removed from her arms but they were black and blue.

'Oh, Jack! I've been waiting for you to come.' She tried to put her arms up to him but the effort was too much and she put them back down.

'Don't exert yourself,' said Jack as he put a hand on her shoulder and kissed her sunken cheek. 'You don't know how good it is to see you.'

'He is evil, Jack. I saw it in his eyes.' Her eyes filled with tears. 'I thought I was a goner.' She breathed out heavily. 'I'm a bit short of breath. Every time I think about it my heart goes crazy. You'll have to be patient with me. Does my make-up look okay? The nurse helped me to do it.'

The nurse looked up and smiled.

'You look beautiful as always. Is there anything you remember about the man who attacked you?'

'Tall, thin, long ginger hair and evil blue eyes,' she said weakly as her voice cracked. 'It was a wig, Jack. Wigs smell different to real hair. There was another smell. Soap. I can't remember what it's called. He leaned over me to tie me up. It was a strong smell. He had a badge with the name Phil on pinned to the front of his boiler suit. I'm so tired, Jack.' Her eyes looked heavy and began to close. 'It's red soap,' she muttered as she lay back on the pillows.

The nurse came to the bed. 'She needs to rest now.'

'I'll be in to see you tomorrow,' said Jack. He kissed her again and left. 'Red soap with a strong smell,' he muttered as he closed the door behind him.

Back at the station, Jack settled in a chair opposite Claude Benson. 'Claude you don't look any older than when I last saw you. Still look like Charlton Heston. How long's it been?'

'Must be over a year Jack. What's all this about? Your gaffer said you wanted to see me about my old Ford Anglia.'

'Not the car, the number plate. Are you aware of the recent abduction on Broad Street?'

'Yes, he told me. A young girl from the library, wasn't it?'

'The car that was used had the same registration number as your Ford Anglia.'

'Yes, he said that too. I don't know anything about that Jack.'

'How long have you had the car, Claude? And where did you get it from?'

'Well, I bought it off a Mrs Cartwright when she got done for drink driving. It was nineteen-ninety-eight. I've checked my records like he asked me to.'

'Where does she live?'

'Down Old Moat. You won't find her though. She died a couple of years after she sold me the car. There was talk that she done herself in because she couldn't get over her son's death. He was a surgeon. It was all over the papers, Jack. They had money.

I could tell you a thing or two about her old man.

He was a surgeon as well. He died about five years before his wife. Anyway, the car was immaculate. I tek it all over the country to classic car meetings. Won prizes for her, I have.'

'How did Mrs Cartwright's son die?'

'Like her, in a fire. He committed suicide as well, so I heard.'

'What about the old man?'

'He had a heart attack. Shagged anything that breathed that one. When I had my garage he was shagging the young receptionist who worked for me.'

Jack smiled. 'Well I don't think that will be relevant to our enquiries at the moment, Claude, as much as I like to hear gossip. What I would like is a list of names and addresses of all the men who work for you.'

'I got that here, Jack. Murray asked me to do it for you.' He pulled a piece of paper from his pocket. 'The taxman will have a field day!'

'You won't be investigated for tax. I need the names of anyone who could have used or got hold of the plates or just been familiar with them. You don't want to be harbouring a kidnapper, or possible murderer, do you?'

'No, Jack. That's a full list of everyone who's worked for me the last five years.

Names and addresses.'

'Thank you, Claude. We need to get DNA samples from all who fit the age group of the suspect.'

'Most of 'em are young, Jack. They have to be

strong and fit to work in scrap.'

'They might all have to be tested then. Thanks for coming in, Claude.'

'While I'm here. I don't know if it's of any relevance, Jack, but someone broke in to the scrap yard two nights ago. The chains were cut through.'

'Did they take anything?'

'Come on, Jack. I don't keep a close eye on all the scrap we've got. It's impossible. They could have taken anything.'

'I was thinking number plates, Claude. The kidnapper might be looking for new ones.'

'I'll do what I can to check but kids are always breaking in and stealing stuff. It's usually only things they can carry and sell for a few bob. I'm putting a dog in there now and a camera.'

'One last thing, Claude. Do any of the men who work for you own a blue Ford Escort?'

'I don't think so, Jack. Most of 'em don't own the shoes they come to work in.'

*

Michael was admiring his costume in the mirror. Another half hour and he'd be up in the battlements with his bow and arrows. The public were invited to dress in costume, so that's what he'd done. He loved the full beard and bushy hair. No-one would recognise him. There would be lots of people with bows and arrows. He'd been practicing for weeks on the fields at the back of the manor. The bow and arrows belonged to his father, the evil bastard. He would shoot rabbits and foxes on their land and bring their bodies home like trophies to feed to his two hounds. 'Silent killing' he called it. He would make Michael watch, and laughed if the boy vomited as he skinned the corpses.

*

Jack woke up with a start. His mobile phone and land line were both ringing. He answered the mobile. 'Jack Riley.'

'Jack you'd better get up to the castle at once. I was sitting right next to her. Missed me by six inches,' Murray sounded out of breath.

'What's up, sir? What are you talking about?'

'Right through her fucking eye, Jack!'

'Whose eye?'

'The Mayoress, Councillor Lloyd! She was sitting next to me. The next thing you know I heard a swish and a bloody arrow went right through her eye. It must be terrorists Jack! Or it was meant for me!'

Chapter Twenty-Four

Thursday morning

The station was hectic. Officers were in and out every few minutes, phones constantly rang and faxes and printers beeped every few seconds. The corridors were full of people eager to tell their version of the events at Dudstone Castle and news reporters were kept at bay by Superintendent Middleton, who deemed the crime serious enough to demand his presence. Nothing like this had happened in Dudstone since medieval times. A local paper's headline boldly stated, 'Mayoress of Dudstone Assassinated!'

'The castle and historic buildings have been closed to the public until further notice,' Middleton told the reporters outside the station. 'All I can say at this time is that the Mayoress, Councillor Lloyd has sustained a fatal injury and we can't rule out that this could be a politically motivated attack by terrorists. I'm asking for the public to be vigilant and report anything they think might be suspicious or anyone they know or suspect could be involved in this attack. Officers from neighbouring towns have been drafted in to help with our enquiries and will be working with us until we find the culprit or culprits who committed this horrendous crime in our community. Thank you for your co-operation in this matter. I will speak to you again when I have more information.'

Jack was behind the desk with Hadley. 'Take their names and addresses Hadley. Anyone who actually saw who shot the arrow is to be interviewed in room one.'

'Yes, sir.'

'I'll be in my office if anyone comes in with anything useful to our enquiries.'

'Yes, sir.'

Murray was in sitting at Jack's desk when he opened the door.

'Good morning, sir. How are you feeling?'

'I'm bloody knackered. I've had no sleep. All leave has been cancelled for the time being, Jack. Superintendent Middleton's holding a press conference this afternoon. He thinks it was a politically motivated attack. Councillor Lloyd is well known for her views on customs and traditions. She was also against the planned new mosque. The demonstration on Saturday has been cancelled.'

'How's the mayor?'

'In bloody shock like me. He's at home with his son and daughter.'

Chapter Twenty-Five

Lily lay on her bed looking at the ceiling. A damp patch had appeared right above her. She tried to make pictures with the shape. It looked like a dwarf when she turned her head to the right, and a rose when she turned to the left. She was always looking for things to occupy her mind, or to take her mind off the inevitable. And that was the birth of her baby. The Doctor hadn't given her anything for the baby. He'd been going on about deformed legs and operations recently. She knew he was talking about himself. She knew if the baby had anything wrong with it, he would operate on it or kill it. She'd seen madness in his eyes so many times, and knew her existence was as delicate as a soap bubble. What fate would her baby have? She couldn't see any kind of future for it, or herself.

Something bumped in another room. The Doctor had been out for more than an hour. It must have been Catherine working on the hole under the sink. The thought that he would catch Catherine scared her to death. If he found out about it he would kill her on the spot. Her stomach rolled over at the thought. The baby kicked as if it sensed her fears. She put her hand on it and started to rub it gently, round and round in circles.

'Here we go round the mulberry bush, on a cold and frosty morning.'

'Lily!'

'Yes, Catherine!'

'It's almost big enough, Lily! I have four bricks out now. I put them back to make it look like they're still solid. They're quite big, Lily! I think another two or three and I'll be able to squeeze through the hole.'

'Catherine, please be careful! I'm so worried he'll find it.'

'He hasn't looked under there since the first day I came here. The cement is so soft it falls out when I move the bricks from side to side, you know like a loose tooth? It's an old building, Lily and the outside walls are crumbling.'

'I do hope you can get out and save us.'

'Don't worry, Lily! We'll be home soon!'

'I don't think I can take much more!'

'Lily! Lily! Be strong, like you told me! We will be going home! I promise you!'

'It's hard to be hopeful, Catherine. I haven't seen daylight for over two years and I feel so weak. I'm terrified of having this baby.'

'Don't give up, Lily! I know we'll make it! I'm never going to give up hope. I want to tell you my terrible secret. I want you to help me decide what to do about it. You're the only person I have in the whole world right now.'

*

He watched the young girl who worked at the greengrocer's. Her name was Emily. He'd called at the shop to buy fruit and heard the owner call to her. He was parked several yards up the road from the shop which, on this bright, warm Thursday evening, was about to close.

Emily stood in the shop doorway and looked up and down the road. Her father was late, as usual. That was the trouble with coming from a large family. She wondered what had happened to make him late and imagined various scenarios. Perhaps Ryan had fallen off his bike again and he was at the hospital getting stitched. Or maybe Chloe had got appendicitis, or Georgia had been sick? Perhaps the dog had got out and they were all out searching for him? She smiled to herself. Sometimes her imagination worked overtime.

Such a pretty little thing, with golden hair and blue eyes. She was thirteen. She would be untouched, virginal. Her tight pink top clung to firm young breasts, just ripening for him to kiss and her cut-off jeans hugged her peachy little backside. She was beautiful. He knew now that if he didn't get a young one, it wasn't worth bothering. The three he'd tried had all been whores. Not one of them had been worthy of taking Rebecca's place. 'Emily', he said to himself and smiled. 'My little Goldilocks.'

Emily stepped out from the shop doorway and looked in the direction her father would come. She sang along to music on her phone. A black car was parked a few yards away along the road and the man inside looked in her direction. She could just make out the registration number of the car, so she put it in her phone and saved it. Emily was suspicious of everyone. Her mother and father had warned her so many times about strangers and what nasty men would do to her if they took her. He watched as the girl looked up and down the road again and played with her phone.

She was waiting for her father. He hoped she would get fed up and start to walk. Teenagers were all the same. They all had those stupid things in their ears to listen to the rubbish that boy bands churned out. Half the time they weren't aware of the world around them. A few yards in front of him the road was no more than a lane to the next village. It would be easy to stop and snatch her along there.

The man had been parked there for more than ten minutes. Emily wondered what he was doing. There were no houses on his side of the road and he didn't appear to be reading a map or newspaper. He was wearing a red baseball cap and dark glasses. She was sure he was watching her, or the shop. Perhaps he was planning to rob Mrs Jones. She wished her father would hurry up. Mrs Jones would lock up and go home in a few minutes. She would be left to wait, all alone. She went back in the shop just as a green Range Rover pulled up outside.

Michael banged his hand on the steering wheel. Emily's father had arrived. He started up the car, turned round and drove off. He hadn't reckoned on her being so patient. He'd have to use other means to get her.

*

Catherine stood with her back to the door. Tears ran down her cheeks. 'It all started when my mother had her first breakdown. We were on holiday in a caravan in Wales. I can't remember the name of the place, I was only eight years old. I don't know why my mother suddenly became ill. She was asleep. My father had given her some pills. He told me to sit by him to watch television. After a few minutes he put his arm round me and began to cuddle me. I giggled. It was something he did often. But then he turned to me and kissed me on the lips. A proper kiss, not a daddy kiss. Then he put his hand in my pants. Oh, Lily! I didn't know what to do.'

'You're not to blame, Catherine. You were an innocent child. You have nothing to be ashamed of.'

'I do Lily, I do! I didn't tell him to stop. When I was twelve he got in to my bed one night and had sex with me. It was so horrible, and painful. He didn't care Lily. I told him to stop then, but he didn't, he just said it was his way of showing how much he loved me. Then he told me if I told anyone I would be sent away and I'd never see my mother again.'

'He's a sick, evil man, Catherine. What he did to you is wrong. You are not to blame. Please believe me. Good fathers don't do that.'

'What shall I do, Lily? What would you do?'

'I would tell my mother. Or someone close to me.'

'I couldn't tell my mother, it would kill her.'

'I think it is best she knows the truth, Catherine.

177

You both need to be away from

that man. I could break my heart for you. Going through all that, having your childhood taken from you and now being abused by someone else. You poor girl.'

'You're so kind, Lily. And so caring. I wish you'd been my friend all my life.'

'I will be your friend from now on Catherine, I promise. I will help you when we get out. I will be there with you when you tell them. If you want me to.'

'Oh, Lily! Thank you. Thank you so much.'

*

Jack and DS Morgan were going through the list of nine names and addresses Claude Benson had given him.

'Seven of them have had DNA tests,' said Jack. 'The other two don't fit the age group of the DNA samples we found on the handkerchief. A couple of them have convictions for burglary and shoplifting, but nothing serious. None have violent records. I'm a bit niggled by something Benson said concerning the previous owner of the car number plate. Mrs Cartwright. He told me she'd committed suicide two years after her son had killed himself. Apparently they'd both been killed in fires started by themselves and her son was a doctor.'

'Would you like me to look in to that?'

'Yes, thanks. I'm going to see Miss Baker. She told me her attacker smelt like strong red soap. Do you have any thoughts on that? I mean there's so many different ones it could be. There's roses or tulips.'

'Carbolic soap. It smells very strong and I believe it's red or sometimes green. It was common in hospitals and institutions, like schools. I don't think it's used by them now though because of the phenol content, it's been replaced with anti-bacterial soap dispensers.'

'Of course. Carbolic. But surely Miss Baker would remember that. She was a school teacher. But she has been getting a little confused lately. Do they still sell it?'

'Hardware stores usually have some, and market stalls. Perhaps supermarkets still sell it. It smells the same as the original carbolic soap but since the late nineteen-eighties they've used tea tree oil.'

'I'll mention it to her. I'm going to see her now. Sandy you have a wealth of knowledge.'

'My grandfather was a surgeon, he always used it. You're not on the case, remember?'

'Officially. How can I stay away from it? She's my friend. I'm only going to ask about soap.'

*

When Jack arrived at the hospital Doctor Bird was waiting outside Miss Baker's room. 'I've just called the station. They told me you were on your way here. It's bad news, I'm afraid. Miss Baker passed away ten minutes ago. It was sudden. I'm sorry I couldn't give you notice so that you could be with her. It was her wish that we shouldn't disclose the full extent of her injuries to you, Mr Riley.'

'What do you mean?'

'She didn't want you to know that she'd been brutally raped in the attack. She said I could tell you if she didn't make it. She ordered me to take swabs for your experts to examine for DNA before she agreed to be operated on. They were from the throat, vagina and anus. I sent them to your colleague Professor O' Brien. I'm sorry there was nothing else we could do for her. Her heart gave up the fight.'

'You could have told me doctor!'

'Patient confidentiality, Inspector Riley. Sorry.'

'You knew she wouldn't survive, didn't you?'

'She had a weak heart. I was hopeful she would survive though.'

'I wouldn't have mentioned it to her. I have too much respect for the lady to embarrass her.'

'I'm sorry but my patient had to come first. It was her wish not to tell you. I had to respect that. No doubt if she'd survived she would have told you herself.'

'Professor O' Brien hasn't told me anything about this.'

'From what I understand you're not actually investigating her attack because of your friendship with her. That's what I was told by Professor O' Brien.'

Jack left the hospital and moved his car to the far end of the car park where no-one could see him. Gwen hadn't told him about the swabs, and he realised why. She'd tried to save him from knowing the worst, she knew it might break him. He put his head in his hands and sobbed for the old lady who had been a wonderful friend to him for the last nine years.

Chapter Twenty-Six

Friday morning

Jack was at the market looking at the goods on Joey Coombs's stall. 'Do you sell carbolic soap, Joey?'

'Down at the far end,' Joey replied. 'Next to the yellow dusters.'

'Do you get many people buying this stuff nowadays?'

'Mainly the old ens. They tend to be stuck back in the fifties and sixties. Me grandad used to scrub his shirt collars and cuffs with it. Reminds me of hospitals though.'

'How much do you sell?'

'Quite a bit. One chap buys it by the box.'

'Oh. Do you know his name?'

'It's bloody soap, Inspector, not cannabis. How can I ask him his name? Oh, by the way, sir, you're buying too much soap, you're too clean and we can't have that. What's your name and address?'

'What does he look like?'

'Clean! How do I know what he looks like? I don't look into his bloody eyes! He's a bloke, he'd think I was queer or something! He's posh. He's a bit young though. Like I said it's usually old folk who buy it.'

Jack took a card from his wallet. 'Phone me when he's here again, Joey.'

'Eff me! What's in the bloody stuff? I'll have to put the price up!'

'It's important to me, Joey. And it might help with the DVD player case against you. I've been told to charge you with receiving stolen goods. That tip you gave me about them going up to Manchester was very useful.'

'What you on about, Mr Riley? I never said nothing about that!'

'I'm trying to help you here, Joey. DS Jones will be coming to see you about it. Any help you can give him will help you.'

'Oh. Okay, Mr Riley. Thanks. I'm not going to put a foot wrong from now on. I don't want to be sent down and leave the missis an kids again.'

'That's good to hear. I hope you stick to it. Don't forget to ring me if the soap man comes.' Jack opened his wallet and counted out a hundred pounds. 'Here. To help with the family and your recent losses. It's between me and you Joey.'

'I couldn't, Mr Riley. I can't take your hard earned cash.'

Jack pushed the money into Joey's hand. 'Take it. I've nothing to spend it on. You behave yourself, Joey. I can see some good in you.'

'Thanks, Mr Riley. I won't let you down.'

Jack turned to walk back through the market stalls.

'Oh, Mr Riley, I just remembered! He's got a limp!'

'What?' Jack swung round.

'Him who comes for the soap. He's got a limp.'

*

He was standing by the statue of a former Earl of Dudstone when he saw Jack Riley talking with the market trader. Riley was giving him money. He took a picture of them on his phone. Perhaps the market trader was one of Riley's snitches. He wouldn't be going there anymore. For a few seconds he panicked when he saw Riley heading his way. The tic below his eye began to twitch. He pretended to be talking on the phone and covered the side of his face with his hand to hide it.

'Nice morning to be out,' said Riley as he passed. 'Have a good day, lads.'

*

Jack and DS Morgan were ready to look at more CCTV footage. There was still a lot to go through. They were in the large office where sixteen computer screens were all switched on. Half of them were occupied by other officers. DS Morgan sat in front of one of them and typed in a password. The screen came to life. Jack got a chair and sat next to her.

'I'm really sorry to hear about your friend, Jack. Are you sure you want to be here?'

'I'm going to find him. It's a murder investigation now. This is where I should be. Murray's in a state over Councillor Lloyd's death. He thinks the arrow was meant for him, but Middleton thinks it was a terrorist attack. We found a rope where he climbed down from the castle and took off into the trees and across the miniature railway track. That leads to the Castle council estate. He could have gone anywhere. Hundreds of people were dressed up.'

'Yes, I was one of them. It was a wonderful night until then. I think we arrested forty people with bows and arrows, but they were toys or theatrical props. The arrow that killed her was a proper one, believe me. There wasn't as much blood as you would think, it…'

'I'd rather not hear anymore thanks. Murray's in charge of that investigation. Let's get on with ours.'

'For someone who sees so much violence in their work you haven't got a very strong stomach have you?'

'Do you have a problem with that, DS Morgan? If you must know I've only had it since Lily went missing. It doesn't affect my work.'

'I don't have a problem with it. I'm sorry for mentioning it. Are we going to carry on where we left off yesterday?'

'We surely are,' said Jack. 'I have a feeling our car is somewhere on these tapes. Wallace is looking at CCTV from the library. Did you find out anything about Amelia's operation?'

'Yes. It was at a clinic in Dublin, and it was to lengthen her leg. Her mother said she was born with lower leg deficiency and had two or three operations as a child, and one when she was older. She also said she got friendly with a young man who had a leg problem, but she didn't know his name. Why are we looking at these tapes?'

'The suspect might be on the tapes. Walking back to the car or round the car park. He might be someone we know. The more evidence we have, the more certain we can be of a conviction. You'd be surprised the loopholes some solicitors find. He would stand out if he has a limp, wouldn't he?'

'Okay. Yes. If he had an operation would he still limp?'

'It depends on how bad the deformity was. We need the dates of Amelia's operations to check out anyone who was having treatment at the clinic at the same time.' Wallace appeared at Jack's shoulder. 'What is it Wallace?'

'There's something you need to see, sir.'

'This had better be important, Wallace.' Jack followed the constable across the room to the computer he'd been working on.

'Here sir, look! This is at one forty-five on the day Catherine Bennett went missing.' The computer screen went black then came back on, then went off again.

'What's up now?' said Jack.

'I don't know, sir. I'll get it up on another one.' Wallace pressed some keys on another computer and the screen flashed on then went black.

'For god's sake what's going on?' said Jack. 'You'd better get someone to fix these.'

'The technician came in this morning to look at them, sir. He might still be here.'

'This one works,' DS Morgan called from across the room.

Wallace went to the computer and got the picture up again.

'Is that who I think it is?' said Jack.

'Yes, sir, it's Lofty… I mean, Constable Hadley.'

'Get him in here, Wallace! He was up by the market place, near the firemen's display, handing out pictures of Catherine Bennett with a few other lads. I saw him on my way in this morning. He's got a lot of explaining to do! Why wasn't this found earlier?'

'I don't know, sir. It should have already been looked at. I was re-checking as you asked me to.'

*

Michael was in a foul mood. Abducting Emily was going to be harder than he thought. He would have to find out where she lived and watch her from there. But now he had to feed the other two. He was getting tired of it. Sometimes he felt so down he just wanted to lock the doors and forget about them. He was glad he hadn't put his grandmother's house up for sale yet. Selling houses attracted a lot of attention and it would take up too much of his time. He still owned one in London. The land on the edge of Bordley, where the other one had burnt to the ground when his parents died, now belonged to someone he knew very well. A new house was being built there. His grandmother's house was the only one where his father hadn't abused him.

He'd stayed there after his parents' death for a week before he was locked away in the place for disturbed children. He would take Emily to one of them when he had her.

The day they broke the news of his grandmother's death he felt jubilant inside, but he had to put on a show for his keepers and cried his heart out. When he went up to his room he punched the air. That was one less he had to worry about when he got out. His grandmother hadn't been right since her son and his wife had died in the house fire and she'd used that has an excuse for not taking him in. She hated him for telling her about the abuse he suffered at the hands of her son, and didn't believe a word he said. It was her fault he was locked up in the first place.

*

Hadley stood in front of Jack, his hands behind his back, his face hot and flustered, beads of sweat formed on his brow.

'What I want to know, is why you didn't tell me you saw Catherine Bennett on the day she went missing!' Jack shouted as he circled the young constable.

'Well, sir… I'd been to ask Catherine for a date… and she… told me she was going out with her friends that night. That's all, sir. I didn't think it…'

'You didn't think! What? You didn't think that as an officer of the law you should have reported your meeting? What are you trying to hide, Hadley? Did you meet her after work? Did you take her off somewhere and kill her when she said no?'

'No, sir! No! I was here, sir. There were reasons why I couldn't say anything. It's her father, sir. He doesn't like her having a boyfriend. He's very strict. I didn't want to cause problems for her.'

'Can you see the mess you've put yourself in by not telling us about meeting Catherine on the day she went missing? Didn't I give you the opportunity to tell me this outside Miss Baker's hospital room?'

'Yes, sir. I realise how it looks. I'm sorry I lied to you.'

'How tall are you, Hadley?' Jack was exasperated.

'Six two, sir.'

'That's about the same height as the man who came to my flat and the man seen at the library.'

'Not me, sir!'

'Sir!' Wallace called across the room. 'I think this is him, the fellow with the limp. He was in the library on Wednesday according to this, two days before Catherine vanished.'

Jack and DS Morgan moved to view the footage on Wallace's screen. He turned to Hadley. 'Blond hair. Just like you. You're a suspect in the kidnapping of Catherine Bennett. Go with Wallace and make a statement. Put him in a cell when you have his statement. Get him out of my sight! And get the damn technician back in here to look at these computers!'

'Sir! It's not me. I have dark brown hair. I dye it.' Hadley called as he walked out with Wallace.

'Sir, do you really think that young man kidnapped Catherine?' DS Morgan stood in front of him as the two constables disappeared into one of the offices. 'Don't you think you were a bit hard on him? He was almost in tears.'

'I've seen baby killers cry DS Morgan. They were still guilty of the crimes they committed. He withheld information. He's also strikingly similar to the bloke on the CCTV. Now he says he dyes his hair, which makes him even more of a suspect. This footage has been marked as seen but no-one's said anything about Hadley being on it. It's a good thing I asked Wallace to re-check it. We'll have a look to see who checked it before Wallace. Murray is suspicious that someone on the team has spoken to the press about the attack on Miss Baker.'

'I'll get the records.'

DS Morgan came back to Jack with a manila folder. 'In here it says Hadley viewed it Jack. Look. Library Friday CCTV. Constable Hadley. Viewed Saturday at 10am.'

'He wasn't here. He went home at eight, he'd been on shift all night. He was making coffee for us all night. I sent him home to get a few hours rest. I want to know who was here after eight on Saturday morning. Get me the shift sheets. I was here but I can't remember what everyone was doing.'

'It will take ages to go through this, Jack,' DS Morgan returned with the sheets.

'Just look at Saturday morning, that's all. How many officers would normally be in?'

DS Morgan scanned the sheets. 'Hundreds,' she handed him the sheet. 'Jack, that was the morning after Catherine went missing.'

'Of course it was. Everyone was called in.'

'There were teams out doing house to house. It

would have been hectic.'

'Yes, that's true, but they all have to sign in. I'm going to take this to Murray, see what he thinks. The rota should tell us who was doing what on Saturday morning. I've a feeling whoever it is won't say they were checking the CCTV at the library. The only other option is that Hadley did view it at another time and put his name to say it was checked so that we wouldn't check it again and see him talking to Catherine. But surely he would have realised that he wasn't in at ten on that Saturday.'

'He might have been in a panic and forgotten.'

'He's a suspect now, we have the evidence. We have him speaking to her on camera. We'll see what he says about it. I can't believe he's involved. He seemed genuinely concerned about the girl when he called me in. He stayed here all night phoning people who knew her. Perhaps it was all just to cover his involvement. I don't know. Let's have a closer look at that image.'

DS Morgan sat in front of the computer and zoomed in on the picture. 'It's only a side view, but you can see clearly that his eyebrows are very dark. That's quite unusual with someone who has blond hair, isn't it?'

'I'm not sure,' said Jack. 'It's only black and white imaging. They do look quite dark though. I'm more convinced now that it's a blond wig and the DNA on the handkerchief is this guy's. The man who attacked Miss Baker wore a long ginger wig. Could it be the same man? If so, he's accustomed to dressing up in disguise. They're the same height. Does he look like anyone we know?'

'I can't really say. It's not a good picture. According to the evidence we have we're looking for a man aged twenty-five to thirty, who's six feet two inches, with dark hair, blue eyes and a possible limp?'

'Yes,' said Jack. 'It sounds just like Hadley, except for the limp. Print it off. Perhaps the limp is to throw people off. Joey Coombs also said the soap buyer has a limp. None of our men limp, do they?'

'I don't know them all, Jack and I've only met a couple of the PCSOs.'

'We'll have another look at the CCTV around the club where Amelia went missing after I've spoken to the chief.'

*

Jack emerged from Murray's office with a serious frown on his face. 'Murray now thinks someone is trying to frame Hadley.'

'What's he going to do about it?'

'We need to get Hadley back in and ask him about the CCTV. This note was found in the end of the arrow that killed Councillor Lloyd.' He put a plastic bag flat on the table. 'What do you make of it?'

DS Morgan read. 'If a priest's daughter defiles herself by becoming a prostitute, she disgraces her father; she must be burned in the fire.'

'Do you think this is referring to Catherine Bennett? A priest's daughter?'

'Yes, I do. He's going to burn her, Jack. We have to find him. I wonder why he's so upset with Catherine?'

'The quote might answer that. He thinks she's a prostitute.'

'He's either raped her or found out she's had sex. She's not suitable for him. He wants a virgin, Jack. These notes indicate that he's someone who's had a strict religious upbringing. They link Amelia's kidnapping and murder to Catherine's abduction and the murder of Councillor Lloyd.'

'Why has he killed Councillor Lloyd? Or was he trying to kill Murray? He's taken Catherine. He killed Amelia. I think he killed Stella. Is there anything that links these people together? Let's get back to the footage around the club. The car registration might be on it somewhere.'

For twenty minutes they sat in silence. 'Stop there!' Jack called out and pointed at the screen. 'There! Zoom in closer. Look! Something… two, then B C Y. That's the number.. well four digits of it. Where is this place?'

'Just off the High Street in Fenlow. Round the corner from the nightclub.'

'Now we have another link in the case.'

'There's no image of a person anywhere near and that car's not a blue escort. It's an Audi, and it's black.'

'Yes, like a taxi. Easy to mistake when you've been on the piss all night.'

'He changes the number plates,' said DS Morgan. 'From one car to another. I suppose this might get Hadley off the hook for Catherine's abduction?'

'No. He's still got to explain the CCTV,' said Jack.

'He should have owned up to meeting her. Personally I don't think he viewed the CCTV footage. I think someone else on the team did and Murray's right about someone trying to frame him. I'm going to check his work rota with the times the suspect was seen at the library. I wonder if Ted remembers who viewed the CCTV on Saturday morning. I think I'll give him a call. What do you make of Catherine Bennett's father?'

'You don't think he kidnapped his own daughter, Jack? He doesn't fit the profile.'

'He seems on edge to me. Hadley said Catherine was afraid of upsetting him, or having a boyfriend. It seems a bit too possessive to me. And we have all these Biblical quotes from the kidnapper. Maybe I'm overthinking. I don't know. I just think he's a bit of a perv.'

'She's an only child. He's bound to be possessive. You seriously think he'd send Biblical quotes, him being a preacher. I don't think he's that stupid, but I'll check him out if it's bothering you. Hadley could have said those things to deflect our attention from himself.'

'Yes, I'm aware of that. Bennett was sweating like a pig at the interview and he was very insistent on Catherine's obedience. I find that strange. Most teenagers are mouthy brats at some point in their growing up. I know I was.'

Jack took his phone from his pocket and pressed Ted's number. 'Ted, I was wondering if you could remember if anyone checked the CCTV footage from the library on Saturday morning after the meeting?'

'Well I know who I told to check it but whether he did or not I'm not sure because I went out on house to house.'

'Who was it Ted?'

'DS Jones.'

'Why am I not surprised?'

'What's happened, Jack?'

'Something was missed. Don't worry about it. I'll see you soon. Bye.'

Chapter Twenty-Seven

While his parents were shopping in town, Steven Munroe found his birth certificate in a drawer in their bedroom. There'd been an air of discomfort in the house since he'd mentioned looking into his past and although he didn't like sneaking round behind their backs, he was determined to know about his real parents. It would be easy to get the information now he had a name. He left the house ten minutes later and headed for the register office in the town centre.

Michael pulled up outside the house at Bordley just as a car backed off the drive. He managed to get a good look at the driver as he pulled away. He could hardly contain himself. The shock made him shake. He took a deep breath, tried to calm himself. The most important part of his plan could be played out. He could now watch Steven Munroe.

On his way home he stopped in the town of Segmore, which bordered Tipley and Dudstone. He parked on the small shoppers' car park at the back of the High Street.

The old Alambra cinema had been converted to a

bistro bar while he'd been away.

Next to it was Chapman's News. The old bastard who owned that was the chairman of the committee that had him locked up. Michael watched him through the window, stocking the shelves behind the counter with cigarettes, dressed in old jeans and a zig-zag patterned jumper. He had grey stubble and greasy hair. He seemed nothing like the arrogant prick who, years ago, had decided a small boy was a danger to the public and should be locked away with criminals. He was next on Michael's list. The shop opened at six every morning. The old man was there at five, sorting out paper rounds. All by himself.

Friday evening

He was parked in a side road near to the greengrocer's. Dressed as a workman in blue overalls and wearing a curly blond wig, he watched Emily as she stood outside the shop. The Audi was now repainted white and had new false number plates.

Emily's father pulled up and she got in. Michael pulled out and followed as they passed the end of the road. They drove along the lane to the next village. He was surprised when they pulled on to the car park of The Prince Albert public house and Emily and her father got out and went inside. She'd never mentioned that in the chat room. There were a dozen or so cars on the car park. He parked in the far corner.

Inside the pub was decorated with pictures from the village's past, lots of cheap looking horse brasses and dark beamed low ceilings. A typical country pub with a blackboard menu that offered home cooked food.

At the bar Emily's father came to serve him. He bought a glass of coke, observed the folk around him and listened to the chatter between Emily's father and his customers. Just before he left he caught a glimpse of Emily in the room behind the bar. Now he knew where she lived it would be easier to watch her movements.

*

'What's our next move, Inspector?' DS Morgan stood in the doorway of Jack's office. 'We need to consider that the first two digits on that number plate might be different to the ones you have. There could be hundreds of combinations.'

'Sergeant Poole is looking for more images of the car. I know it's not a one hundred per cent certainty. It's a gut feeling. It seems logical this was the car used to abduct Amelia. It's too much of a coincidence that a car with the same number plate is parked right next to the club where she was last seen. I've checked with the men who were in on the Saturday morning after Catherine Bennett was abducted. They were all doing what they were supposed to be doing on the log sheet. Extra PCSOs were called in to man the desk because everyone else was busy. Jones said he checked the CCTV at the library from five-thirty when Catherine was seen leaving. We don't know who viewed it for Friday lunch time and put Hadley's name to it. Someone did. If they have nothing to hide why haven't they admitted it?'

'You're thinking it's Jones, aren't you? Hadley

could still have viewed it. Like you said to stop us finding out he'd spoken Catherine on the day she went missing.'

'He says he didn't check it. I think he's guilty of being in love with the girl, that's all. And he should have told us. I think Murray wants to believe the kid's innocent. I didn't mention that Hadley said he was asking Catherine out on a date. I thought it might incriminate him, but he's done a good job of that himself now. Jones would have reported it. He loves to get people in the shit. The kidnapper kept Amelia for three years. Lily is still alive. I know she is. I also know her time is running out. We have to catch him, Sandy. My girl's life depends on it.'

'What makes you so sure he's got Lily?'

'This is just between us, Sandy. I'll be for the high jump if you tell anyone else.'

'What?'

'I found Lily's ring in my flat the day after Miss Baker was attacked. The kidnapper must have put it there. The ring links the cases together, so I'd be off the case. Murray won't let me investigate Lily's disappearance, or Miss Baker's attack. I can only investigate the Bennett and Stevens' cases.'

'I still think he should know about the ring, Jack.'

'I will tell him. Just give me a couple more days.'

'She was wearing the ring when she disappeared, wasn't she? Couldn't it have been there all the time?'

'She never took it off. I can't believe it's been lying by the door for over two years, but I can't be a hundred per cent sure she was wearing it.'

'He's either getting desperate or too cocky. And he's obviously taunting you, Jack. He wants your attention.'

'Well he's got that!'

'I've been looking at the file on Mrs Cartwright and I showed it to Gwen.'

'What does she think?'

'She actually told me she wasn't convinced it was suicide.'

'Why does she think that?' Jack gave her a long look and wondered if Gwen had told her about their past. He decided to let it go.

'There was no note, no illness and no real motive. The old woman was a known drunk. The bed had been slept in and her slippers were still by her bed. Wouldn't she have put them on to go downstairs? Here are the case notes.' She handed the folder to him.

'It wouldn't matter if her feet were cold if she was going to kill herself anyway.'

He opened the folder and began to read. 'Why go to bed and come back down? It sounds like a spur of the moment decision. Or maybe she heard something downstairs.'

'She'd made arrangements to have a new kitchen fitted. Does that sound like someone who wants to die? The coroner recorded a verdict of suicide because of the lack of proof pointing towards anything other than suicide. And if it was on the spur of the moment, how come she'd got the petrol ready in the kitchen. Her shoes were by the kitchen door, they were clean. It had rained that night. There was no sign on the kitchen floor that she'd gone outside, no footmarks, nothing. Unless she cleaned it before she set fire to herself. Surely she wouldn't be that fussy if she was just going to lie there and strike a match? There was a stain on the garage floor where the petrol can was normally stored. If she brought it into the kitchen she planned to use it.'

'Or someone else did.' Jack studied the notes. 'Someone could have cleaned the floor before they set fire to her. She'd also got a fractured skull. How would she get that? Now that's a bit suspicious.'

'She was a drunk. She could have fallen.'

'If she fractured her skull when she fell how would she strike a match? Wouldn't she be unconscious?' Jack handed the notes back to DS Morgan.

'She could have been conscious for a few minutes. I've been round to her house. It's a rundown detached four bed residence. Quite up market at one time. She must have had a lot of money to buy a place like that. I knocked on a neighbour's door. She said the kitchen fitters arrived two weeks after the old woman died. They had to go away of course, but she said they were a company called Glassdale. She also said no-one had visited the old woman for years, but recently she'd seen a young man removing boxes and old furniture.'

'My, my, you have been busy,' Jack smiled. 'Another link there could be to the case is if it's someone who works at the scrap yard. We're still waiting for DNA results. The car has been with someone else for about fifteen years.'

'Old Mr Cartwright had been a surgeon and so had his son. I think that gives us a stronger link, Jack.'

Jack stood up and moved towards the door. 'Because the kidnapper operates on his victims.'

'Yes.'

'It's something we should consider. Do you think there could be two kidnappers?'

'There could be. I don't think there are though. We've only found one person's DNA, excluding the victim's of course. They're having problems at the lab with the samples from the plastic sheet. They could have been from someone on the SOC team. Maybe Hadley's DNA should be checked.'

'I think you might be right about that. To put his mind at rest. I wonder who's leaking to the press and messing with the computers?'

'I don't know. Perhaps someone told a friend or made a mistake with the CCTV. It would have been hectic the Saturday morning after Catherine went missing. Mistakes are made. And the computers are on their last legs.'

'Perhaps it's the ghost of the chimney sweep, Jackie Smith. Do you fancy a drink? Or something to eat?'

'I could eat a horse, I've had nothing since breakfast.'

'That sounds encouraging!' Jack laughed. 'At this rate you might put on a bit of weight. Maybe you'll be tempted by the steak and ale pie.'

*

Sandy had finished eating her pie and watched as Jack scraped his dish of apple pie and custard. 'Are you going to eat that dish?'

Jack looked at her then back to the dish. He put his spoon down. 'I was hungry.

I've called a meeting at the station tomorrow morning to bring everyone up to date with what we have so far. Hadley's coming in to talk to the chief after the meeting.'

'Oh right. I'll be there. I was wondering if the young man the neighbour saw was a relative of Mrs Cartwright. She was identified by dental records. There would be a record of who claimed the body for burial or cremation, wouldn't there?'

'She'd already been cremated.' Jack said flat.

'That's not very nice!'

'Sorry.'

'Well, if she's got relatives they would be familiar with that car, wouldn't they?

Just like the blokes from the scrap yard. So they could be suspects as well, don't you think? It's a bit of a coincidence that they all died in house fires, isn't it? Who would be going to her house now?'

'Yes, I suppose it is possible he's a relative and he found the old number plates.'

'You never know,' she yawned. 'Think I'm about ready for bed. What about you?'

Jack raised his eyebrows.

'I... I... don't mean that in any forward way... I mean ... I'm not making...'

'A pass at me?' Jacked interrupted.

'No, I'm not… I...'

'Okay. So you don't fancy me. That's fine.'

'I didn't say that… I…'

'What?' Jack interrupted again.

'You can come back to my place,' she blurted, and looked away before adding, 'just for a coffee.'

Jack nearly fell off his chair.

Chapter Twenty-Eight

Catherine lay on the bed, exhausted from her efforts with the loose bricks under the sink. She'd taken advantage of the Doctor's long absence and had been crouched on her knees for hours. The only downside to his absence was that he hadn't brought her any food, and she was starving. The hole was almost large enough for her to crawl through. The handle of the mop had worn down a few inches with all the prodding and scraping. She hoped the Doctor wouldn't notice it propped behind the broom in the corner. She imagined a reunion with her mother. Her eyes filled with tears. If he found the hole now he would kill her. She got up and went to the door.

'Lily! Lily, are you there?'

'Yes, I'm here, Catherine!'

'There's five out now. Just one more, Lily and I'll be able to get out!'

'I'm so scared, Catherine! I'm having a really bad day. I keep thinking something will happen and we won't be saved. Sometimes I think it would be better if I was dead!'

'Don't say that! We will be saved, Lily! Don't say it! Don't even think it!'

'I'm sorry! I feel so ill, Catherine! I can't see an end to this!'

'Lily! Listen to me! We are going to be okay! I promise you! Please don't give up! You kept me going, now I want to keep you going. We are going home!'

Lily had gone back to lie on the bed. She closed her eyes. She couldn't hear Catherine anymore.

*

Michael got himself a coke and sat on a table near the bar so that he could keep an eager eye on the comings and goings of Emily and her mother as they delivered food to the diners. He was himself tonight, short black hair parted on the left side, blue eyes, a two-day stubble and a fixed smile. The wig, the limp and the glasses were gone. He'd even used the Ford Focus to get here. If Emily had clocked him in the Audi, he had to be as different as he could be while he was in the pub. He wouldn't do anything to make her suspicious. In fact he thought it might be an advantage if she got to know him as a customer. He would be a familiar, friendly face, a person who she might trust if he offered her a lift. Little Goldilocks had no idea he'd been chatting to her on the web for over six months.

Emily delivered his beef sandwich and smiled.

She is so perfect, he thought. 'Thank you, my dear.'

*

'Do you take sugar?' Sandy stood in the doorway of

her kitchen.

Jack was sitting on a green leather settee in the neat lounge. Sandy Morgan was certainly a tidy person. There were no flutters, no cardigans strewn on the settee, no used coffee cups, nothing that could even remotely be considered a mess.

There were three framed photographs along an ornamental fire surround. One of Sandy's graduation, showing her with two other girls, one with an older couple and one with one of the girls who was on the graduation photograph.

'Two please. Nice place you have here. It's so... tidy.'

That morning he'd left his bed was unmade, two or three cups on his coffee table and newspapers and books on the floor by his armchair.

'I'm a bit of a freak,' Sandy confessed, as she put a tray on the table. 'I mean a clean freak. Have you seen the film *Sleeping with the Enemy*?'

'I'm not sure.'

'Julia Roberts and Patrick Birkin. He's a freak, he straightens bath towels and puts all his food tins in a line. He doesn't like mess.'

'OCD,' Jack smiled.

'Yes. That's me.'

Jack's phone rang. 'Ted. How are you? You're back home? That's good. I'll come round to see you in the morning.' He turned away. 'No, she's doing okay.'

He closed the phone and turned to Sandy. 'That

was Ted Bateman. He'll be back on the job in a couple of weeks.'

'I suppose they'll be shuffling me back to Yorkshire.'

'What do you mean?'

'Murray said I was only here because you were short staffed. With Ted coming back I'll be surplus to requirements, won't I?'

'We were short staffed before Ted was ill. We need you on the case. You can't go till we find our man.'

'Thanks for your support, but I don't think Murray will see it that way.' She took a sip from her cup. 'Who's doing okay?'

'Erm… you are…' Jack mumbled.

'I've never met Ted. Why would he ask about me?'

'Well, I did tell him a bit about you.'

'What bit did you mention?'

Jack smiled meekly. 'I… er… told him you had red hair and you were a girl guide.'

'I see,' Sandy stood up and turned away from him. 'I hope the two of you had a good laugh about it! Seems to me everyone is afraid of women who have ambition. The door's behind you, Jack.'

'It wasn't meant as a criticism,' Jack protested. 'I was only making conversation, trying to cheer Ted up. It's nothing at all to do with ambition.' He moved towards her and touched her arm. 'Come on, it's not…'

Sandy stepped back quickly. 'But you still had a

good laugh, eh Jack? Don't you dare try to kiss me!'

'I wasn't going kiss you! The comment to Ted was meant in jest and I'm sorry if...'

'Marty Feldman! That's who you remind me of!'

'He's bloody ugly!' Jack opened the door and left.

Chapter Twenty-Nine

Steven Munroe felt an agitation in his stomach. The note had been left on his car during the night. He instinctively knew that it was genuine. He'd been to the register office and obtained the certificates he needed to prove where he came from and what happened to his family. The directions on the note told him to go to a park in Dudstone. He could hardly contain his excitement as he waited in his car. Suddenly a tap on the side window made him jump from his thoughts.

*

Michael was in a good mood as he made food for the girls. He wasn't bothered that they'd had nothing to eat since the day before. All they were getting now was a plate of cold baked beans and a slice of stale bread. The disappointment he'd felt about Catherine had hit him hard. He'd gone into a depression, which had only lifted when he found the old photographs. Now he had something to look forward to. He knew he would have to get rid of both girls, but right now he was all fired up to execute the next stage of his plan.

Catherine had been subdued since he'd punished her, but if she thought he was off guard, she was mistaken. She did all she could not to look at him when he took the food in, but he could tell she had something on her mind. Whatever it was he hadn't the time to worry about it now, he couldn't be late. He would go in his Ford Focus, but he would put false plates on. He would also wear a disguise, a beard, spectacles and long brown hair. If he had to wait a long time his number might be clocked by someone he knew or by one of the cameras and this was the car he used for work. He didn't want to be caught, just yet.

*

Jack was at his flat looking through Amelia Stevens' case notes and a copy of the autopsy results that Gwen had faxed him. He was about to call her when his phone rang.

It was Murray. 'Jack!'

'Yes, sir.'

'What's this I hear about Hadley having a relationship with Catherine Bennett? Why wasn't I informed about it when you spoke to him about the CCTV footage?'

'I've dealt with him. It's not a relationship, it was more a friendship.'

'We can't afford to have one of our men in the frame for kidnap, or murder. I was willing to give him the benefit of the doubt about speaking with the girl on the day she went missing, but a relationship's a different matter. It puts him right in the frame.'

'Well it's not exactly a relationship, sir. He's a decent young man, and a good policeman. I've suspended him for not disclosing that he met and spoke with Catherine Bennett on the day she went missing. He was at work when she was taken.'

'But he could be in league with the kidnapper! Just because he's one of us it doesn't mean we don't do things properly, Jack.'

'I admit he made a mistake and he should be punished for it. I don't think he's involved with the kidnapping in any way.'

'He didn't tell you he had been arranging a date with the girl on the day she went missing?'

'Well yes, he did. She told him she was busy that night. Sir, I think he's in love with the girl. He didn't want to upset her father. He's the possessive type.'

'How do we know she told him that? He could have set it up for someone else to meet her after work that evening.'

'I don't think he did.'

You don't think! Well, I don't like it. I don't like it at all. He could also be the one who's leaking to the press. I think we should have him back in and do a thorough check on him.'

'He's coming in today to speak to you, sir. You'll get my report. I think it's someone else on the team.'

'For fuck's sake! I hope you're not implying it's DS Jones! I've heard about the flare ups between you two. And the files and notes that were in the wrong folder on Jones's desk. Put there by you, I suspect! It's not good for the morale of the men. And I don't want to hear of any more arguments between you and Jones or I'll suspend both of you! Hadley's DNA will be checked for elimination purposes.'

The phone went dead.

*

PC Andrew Hadley had a lot on his mind on his way to the station. He hadn't meant to mislead his colleagues. He knew his meeting and chatting with Catherine had nothing to do with her kidnapping, but he'd been afraid to own up to it because it would have meant he'd be off the case. In the end that's exactly how it turned out. Now he wished he'd told Jack Riley about the meeting. He wondered who'd found the images of him speaking to Catherine on the CCTV and put his name to it. There was also there matter of his phone. Someone had broken into the locker at the gym and stolen it. He would have to tell DCI Murray about that.

He was driving along Broad Street when he noticed a grey Vauxhall Meriva parked near the entrance to the park. He pulled up on the opposite side of the road. The driver was looking round, as if expecting someone. Hadley thought he seemed anxious and decided to check him out. He took out his notebook and wrote the colour, make and registration number of the car and the time. This could be the kidnapper, returning to the scene to relive the feelings of triumph over again. Hadley had read cases like that, and thought perhaps he could make up for the mistake he'd made. He got out the car, walked across the road and tapped on the window of the grey Meriva.

Steven Munroe opened the window.

'I'm a police officer. Can I ask you what you are doing here, sir?'

'I'm meeting someone,' said Steven.

'You look like someone I know,' said Hadley.

'As a matter of fact, I'm…' Steven noticed someone was coming up behind Hadley.

*

Michael was parked further along the road. When he saw Hadley he got out of the car, opened the boot and picked up a jack handle.

*

Jack turned Lily's ring round in his fingers. He'd studied the prints of CCTV from outside showing the man in the baseball cap and boiler suit. The pictures weren't very good. It could have been anyone. All they could determine was his height. The baseball cap was pulled down and long ginger hair obscured his face. There was only one door into the flats and the fire escape round the back, but anyone who tried to get in at the back would have to get through the gates and would probably set off the alarms at the back of the tailor's shop. He convinced himself the flats were safe from further intrusion. He thought about DS Morgan and the way she'd thrown him out of her flat the night before, despite him apologising for what he'd said. He didn't blame her really, and wondered why men are such idiots when it came to women. She was very attractive and the thought had crossed his mind to kiss her. She'd been so right. He picked up the files he'd brought home and headed out the door to work.

*

Hadley turned and saw Michael…

Michael struck him a hard blow on the side of his head and Hadley dropped to the ground. A pool of blood spread across the road.

'Go quickly!' Michael shouted to Steven. 'Come to the manor. I will explain everything.' He turned, ran back to his car and drove away.

Halfway between the park and the library he took a left turn, did a three point turn and waited for Steven's car to pass the end of the road. As Steven passed he pulled out and overtook him by the library.

Chapter Thirty

Lily stood up. Water ran down her legs and pooled round her bare feet. The baby was coming. The ache in her lower back had changed. It came in spasms every few minutes. She was having contractions. She couldn't cry out. Even if she wanted to cry, she wouldn't. If he knew the baby had come he would take it away. No matter how bad the pain became, she had to be quiet. She'd seen films about childbirth on television. The contractions were getting stronger and closer together. She lay back down on the bed and bit into the pillow as the pain came again.

*

Michael drove back to the manor after he'd hit Hadley and put his car in the garage. There was no CCTV or speed cameras after he left the town, but there would be images of his Ford in the town, and he was glad he'd put false plates on now. He had other plans to execute before he let them know who he was. Fed up of waiting for Steven to arrive and in a state of high anxiety, he went out to fetch the morning paper on his father's old motorcycle.

*

Mr Chapman was sorting through a pile of magazines when he went in. There were no other customers and the old man been very obliging and let him have the paper for free. He managed to find one that hadn't any blood on it.

There were pictures in the paper of the type of cars he'd used to get Catherine and Amelia and CCTV images of him in and around the library. He wondered if they'd found Hadley yet. Someone was bound to have passed through the area by now.

Unless Steven had betrayed him. The thought made his stomach churn. They could be coming for him right now. Surely if he had they would be here by now.

He switched the television news channel on. He'd panicked. The fucking police were there trying to spoil it for him. But he should have stopped to make sure Hadley was dead. There was nothing about Hadley on the news, so why was Steven taking his time to get here. He'd left the gates open for him to drive in. What if he didn't show up at all? His plans were falling apart. Perhaps he should hide the Escort and the Audi for the time being. He went outside and took the fence down, then drove the cars as far as he could into the field at the back of the property. The fence would hide them.

When he put the fence back up he left one panel out. Then he went back in to the field and dug a large hole. He put a can of petrol and a lighter near it. It didn't matter if the girls saw him now, they were never going to leave this house. He wouldn't feed them. He was sick and tired of everything to do with this place. He looked at his watch. Twelve o'clock and Steven still hadn't shown up.

The midday news came on. The attack on Hadley was the main content now. There were shots of the park, with a mention to the abductions of Catherine Bennett, Lily Riley and Amelia Stevens, and a close-up of Superintendent Middleton as he pushed his way through the crowd outside Dudstone police station.

He'd almost been caught by Wallace when he planted the microphone in the investigation room yesterday. He switched it on. They were having a meeting any time now. Hadley's phone was on the table, switched off. It had been easy to get it.

He'd followed Hadley to the gym, in disguise, and waited for him to get in the pool.

Everything had dropped nicely into place. Hadley was their prime suspect now.

*

Catherine had been sick that morning and didn't know where she found the strength to dislodge the last brick. The hole was big enough for her to get through.

The doctor had been outside making a lot of noise, which had drowned out any noise she'd made moving the bricks. It had gone quiet now, but when she poked her head out he was standing right in front of her.

Chapter Thirty-One

'Well, the shit has well and truly hit the fan!' Murray was in Jack's office. 'I don't know all the details but Hadley's lying in a coma with his parents at his bedside. It happened on Broad Street. Looks like someone hit him so hard it cracked his skull, then he fell and cracked it again. Some of his teeth were found twelve feet away in the grass round the park.' Murray rubbed his chest and belched. 'Sorry about that.'

'Any witnesses to what happened?'

'Not sure. He had the sense to write details of a car and the time in his notebook before he was attacked and he left that in his car. It was a grey Vauxhall Meriva. Sergeant Poole checked the ownership. Apparently he's a doctor. I've sent officers to his address but they've called in to say he's not there and his parents said he was on leave from the hospital and had gone camping in North Wales.'

'A doctor? Did he check his place of work?'

'He works at Conley. They confirmed he was on

holiday. They don't know where.' Murray got a cup of water from the cooler and took some pills. He sat down. 'Stomach's giving me hell.' He belched again.

'Why would anyone attack Hadley?'

'I'll tell you why! His DNA matches that found on the handkerchief that was found by the park. He's in on it, Jack, and we missed it. The CCTV of him talking with the girl was missed. He must have checked it himself. I also think if a doctor had seen the attack he would have done something to help Hadley. So this doctor might be the other one and they've had a falling out over something. There's something else I want to show you. He took his phone from his pocket pressed a few buttons then handed it to Jack. 'A photo of you giving money to the market trader.'

Jack stammered. 'W…What? I… I was paying for goods I'd bought.'

'Pull the other one, Jack! How many more cock-ups are we going to have on this case? It's been sent to the fucking newspapers. This is to discredit you and the mobile phone it came from is registered to Constable Hadley. Can you explain that?'

'He was one of the group I saw near the statue the other day. It was the day we found the CCTV footage of him talking to Catherine Bennett outside the library.'

There was a lot of noise in the investigation room when Jack went in. DS Morgan sat near the front of the room with a pile of papers on her lap. She didn't look at him.

Superintendent Middleton stood at the back of the

room with his arms folded across his chest. DCI Murray was in front of the case board studying it closely. He coughed, then turned round to face the group.

'Come on, let's have a bit of quiet now!' The room hushed. 'Detective Inspector Riley is going to bring us up to date with what's happening in the Catherine Bennett case. Feel free to offer any ideas or any new information you've discovered, Jack.'

He motioned Jack to come to the front of the room. 'Before you start, Jack, I have some bad news. Constable Hadley was attacked on Broad Street this morning. He had his notebook on him and clocked a car in the area around the time he was assaulted. I've sent officers to bring the driver here for questioning. We've had no luck finding him at his address or work place so I'm going to hold a press conference later to appeal to him to come forward to assist with our enquiries.'

'How is Hadley, sir?' DS Jones asked.

'He's in a bad way,' replied Murray. 'He's also become a prime suspect in the abduction of Catherine Bennett. Carry on, Jack.'

The room fell silent as the men looked at one another with disbelief and shock on their faces.

'The other suspect in Catherine's abduction and the abduction and murder of Amelia is a white male, aged twenty-five to thirty,' said Jack. 'He has dark brown hair, blue eyes and a possible limp. We think he was the young man seen in the library for weeks before Catherine disappeared. We have a picture here, not a very good one, of him sitting in the reading room of the library. As you can see from this his hair is blond. It's likely he was wearing a wig. I've ruled out the possibility of this being Hadley because at the times he was seen at the library Hadley was at work. I've personally checked the rotas and time sheets.'

'Sir!' DS Morgan held up her hand.

'Yes, DS Morgan,' said Jack.

'I've been looking at the statistics for this combination of colouring. Blond haired people very often have darker eyebrows and eyelashes. It's common in many of these people for their hair to go darker as they get older, but not always, sir.'

'Thank you, DS Morgan. So you're saying the young man at the library might not be the suspect?'

'No, sir, I'm confirming what you think, that he was wearing a wig. The young man hasn't been back to the library since Catherine disappeared. So that makes me believe he's the suspect, sir.'

'Thank you. Anything else you'd like to add DS Morgan?'

'Not at the moment, sir.'

'Okay,' said Jack. 'We learned today that the handkerchief found near the park belonged to Constable Hadley. He was at work at the time of the kidnapping, so he either dropped it at another time or the person who took Catherine Bennett left it there to incriminate him. Constable Hadley has insisted he had nothing to do with the abduction of Catherine Bennett. At the moment he's not able to help us any further with our investigation. Now we come to Amelia's case. According to Amelia's parents she had several operations on her leg to lengthen the bone. She had a limp, the suspect has a limp. They could have met while having operations when they were younger and this could be the reason she got in the car near the club and went with him. We found a black Audi car on the car park near the club and the registration number we could see was the same as the one given to us by Mrs White at the time of Catherine Bennett's abduction. Amelia's last operation was at age seventeen at a clinic in Dublin. We are going to do some checks there to find the names of any young men who were having treatment at the same time. We think the suspect has medical knowledge and has had a strict religious upbringing, which is evident in the notes he's sent us. All of them are passages from the Bible. They link Catherine Bennett's abduction and Amelia's abduction and murder to the same man. The samples from the plastic sheet wrapped round Amelia were inconclusive. That's all so far.'

Murray moved to Jack's side. 'Thank you, Inspector Riley. We have the results of the DNA from swabs taken from Miss Baker. It's not the same as the DNA found on the handkerchief. Miss Baker told Inspector Riley that her attacker wore a long ginger wig, had blue eyes, had a name badge pinned to his chest with the name Phil on and smelled of carbolic soap. It's possible he bought the soap from a trader on Dudstone market. The trader, Joey Coombs, informed us that the man who bought the soap had a limp. I'm not sure how reliable this information is. Joey Coombs has been in trouble a few times in the past and a description of the man who was seen at the library had already been in the newspaper. The notes we've received also link the murder of Councillor Lloyd to the Amelia Stevens and Catherine Bennett cases. If he's the same man who killed Miss Baker we have a serial killer on our hands. We have to catch him before he strikes again. At the moment we don't want anything about Constable Hadley's involvement in the Catherine Bennett abduction leaked to the press. Superintendent Middleton is going to oversee that aspect of the investigation.

Middleton moved to the front of the room. 'I want Constable Hadley's involvement in this case checked and checked again. DI Riley has already done some work on the timescale and Hadley's work rota. I'm sending a team to his home to see if there's any evidence of him being involved in these kidnappings and murders. His parents are obviously distraught over what's happened to him, as we all are. I have no wish to traumatise them any further. We have to gather evidence to prove his innocence or guilt. I will be going with the team to ensure they receive the utmost respect throughout our enquiries.'

There was a lot of noise and chair shuffling as the men stood and filed out of the room.

'Were there any prints on the note from the arrow?' Jack asked Murray.

'No, same paper as the other notes we've had. None on the arrow either. The rope's gone for analysis. I should hear something later today. I think he's got Lily too. I think you've been right all along, Jack.'

'Well there's something I'd like to tell you, sir.'

'If you've got a concrete link to Lily's disappearance

you know you're off the case, don't you?'

'Well, sir, I need to...'

'Sir!' Sergeant Poole called from the door. 'We've just had a call from Segmore Station. A newsagent has been found dead in his shop. His throat was cut!'

Chapter Thirty-Two

Steven Munroe had been parked at the bottom end of the town, near the unused cricket ground all morning. He'd driven off in shock after the young man had been attacked. He couldn't understand why it had happened, or why he'd left the young man in the road. He was a doctor, he was supposed to help people, not leave them to die.

They weren't nightmares he was having now. He was wide awake. They were memories of his early life, opening up parts of his mind that had been sealed for years.

Two boys tip-toed along a dark landing and crept slowly down the stairs. They held hands. They couldn't move quickly because one limped.

'Where we going, Mark?' whispered David.

'We're going to do them in,' Mark replied.

'Who?'

'Mother and Father. We're going to burn the house down. They're both ginned up in the lounge.'

'We can't do that, Mark. There's no-one to look after us.'

The sound of a car horn brought him from his thoughts. 'We killed our parents,' he murmured. 'We set fire to the house.'

The night came back to him now. They'd gone to the kitchen to get matches and paper. Mark lit the paper and set fire to the curtains in the hall. He'd tried to stop him but Mark had pushed him away. He couldn't remember anything after that. When he woke up he was in the hospital. He never saw Mark again. He had to go to the manor and find out what was going on.

*

The baby was a girl. Lily had torn a piece cloth from the hem of her robe and tied it tightly around the cord. Then she'd bitten through the cord to detach it from the baby. She put some of the afterbirth down the toilet but there was too much. The toilet might get blocked if she put it down too quickly and the Doctor would hear her flushing the chain. He would know what had happened. She put it in the mop bucket and covered it with the bloodstained sheet and robe. She washed and changed her clothes. The doctor would expect to see washing so she put a set of clean ones in the sink to make them wet and put them on the radiator. Terror ran through her veins as she put the mop bucket in the cupboard under the sink.

The baby had cried a little, but she was sleeping now. She was lying under the sheet in the middle of the bed Lily was thankful the doctor had been hammering outside all morning and wouldn't have heard her. Where could she hide the baby?

She looked round the room. There was only the small drawer under the sink. She could hear the doctor as he moved round the house and muttered to himself. It was only a matter of time before he realised what had happened. He would take her baby.

She would have to do something to stop her suffering. Tears ran down her face as she put her hand over the baby's mouth and nose.

*

Catherine almost screamed when she saw the man standing with his back to her. He was wearing a blue t-shirt and black jeans. It had to be the Doctor. He was putting a fence panel up at the back of the house. If he turned now she was as good as dead.

Her heart pounded as she quickly replaced the bricks in the hole. She was grateful for the weeds, nettles and long grass that hid her escape route from his view.

The Doctor was back inside the house. Catherine could hear him as he opened and closed doors. She wondered if he would feed her today. She was starving but a part of her wished he wouldn't come in today. If he searched the room now he would find the loose bricks under the sink and kill her. She knew he was going to kill her anyway, or let her die a long lingering death through starvation. She had no doubt about that.

The room was as clean as she could make it. Her washing was drying on the radiator. There was nothing to do now but wait.

*

The sinister tones of funeral music began.

He was outside the room. She could feel his eyes watching her through the peephole. The bolts slid off.

'I've come to bid you goodbye, Catherine.' He stood in the doorway. The Doctor's voice, but his hair was dark and he had a short beard. He came to the bed. 'Yes, you can look at me now. This is the real me, Catherine.'

Catherine glanced at the open door and wondered if she should make a dash for freedom.

'I wouldn't if I were you. The whole house is locked up. You can run if you want to but you won't get out.' He smiled. 'It's my last time with you, so I'm going to have some fun before you go.' He put his hand on her thigh. 'You are a temptress, Catherine. I know what you want me to do. You want to feel me throbbing inside you, don't you?'

'Yes, Doctor,' said Catherine. 'That's what I want.'

The Doctor withdrew his hand quickly, a look of horror on his face. 'What? Are you trying to trick me? It won't work, Catherine. You're supposed to fucking beg for forgiveness you bitch, not fucking seduce me! You little snake! You think being nice to me will save you? Well I'm so sorry, but it won't. Nothing will now. You are as good as dead. So lie still or fight if you want to. Either way you're fucked!' He laughed. 'In every way you can imagine, my dear. Now let's see how far we can get this inside your unholy body.' He was holding the wooden police truncheon. 'The tool of obedience.'

Lily heard the Doctor shout, then laugh loudly. A funeral dirge played in the background. She took her hand from the baby's face. She couldn't hurt her. She lifted the tiny child off the bed and put her in the drawer under the sink.

The Doctor shouted again. Then a scream that made her blood run cold. What was he doing to Catherine? She got under the sheet and drew her knees up to her chest. How long would it be before he came to her? She started to count.

*

The Doctor was exhausted when he'd finished with Catherine. She was lying unconscious on the bed. She hadn't any fight left in her. She wouldn't be going anywhere except to meet her maker. He closed the door and slid the bolts across. He looked at his watch. He was so tired. He would sleep for a while before he went in to the other one.

*

Jack was sat at his desk looking over case files when there was a knock on his door. 'Come in!'

'I wasn't sure what to do, sir. There's a woman on the phone saying she's your wife. I thought I'd better check with you first.' Constable Wallace stood in the doorway.

'My what?' Jack shouted.

'Your wife, sir.'

*

Catherine opened her eyes. She moved and felt pain tear right through her body. The Doctor had raped her and beaten her with a club. She didn't know how long the torture had lasted. It seemed like forever before she passed out. She was alive and had a chance. She struggled to sit up. Her left wrist was swollen and red. It was broken. How would she lift the bricks out? She had to go now. She had to get away.

The house was deathly quiet. He must have gone out. Catherine staggered across the room to the sink and crouched down. Every bone in her body ached. She opened the door and leaned in. The bricks might drop out if she pushed hard enough. She put her right hand on them and pushed with all the strength she had. The bricks fell through the gap and daylight rushed in.

As she twisted her body through the hole her broken wrist cracked again. The pain shot up her arm and down to her fingers, tears ran down her cheeks, she panted. She was out. Her eyes rested on the gap in the fence. She could see fields that stretched as far as she could see. She picked herself up and stumbled towards the gap. One small step at a time. She had to go now, or lie down and die.

A few feet in to the field she fell in a hole. He'd dug her grave. Her heart started to race. Panic took over. She couldn't breathe. 'God help me!' She screamed as she clawed desperately at the soil with her right hand. She managed to climb half way out, but fell sideways and slid back down on her knees.

Chapter Thirty-Three

'Jack?' Susan's voice. 'Are you there, Jack?'

'What do you want?' Jack asked after a long silence.

'Is it right you've found a body? I've heard things.'

'It wasn't Lily,' Jack answered.

'You could let me know these things personally, Jack. Instead I'm just left to wonder what's going on. She is my daughter.'

'Oh, she's your daughter, is she? Well where were you when she was growing up?'

'I haven't called to argue, Jack. I just wanted to know for sure it wasn't Lily. At least I can hang on to a bit of hope.'

'Hope? And what is that?'

'Look Jack, I'm back in England. The business has crashed. Could you put me up for a few days until I find somewhere?'

Jack couldn't believe what he was hearing.

'I want to make peace with you. Jack? Are you still

there?'

'Yes, I'm here. What's happened to good old Jeff then?'

'He's left me. I need your help, Jack. Please!'

Murray appeared in the doorway just has Jack put the phone down. 'You okay, Riley? You look a bit shell shocked.'

'Susan's back from Spain. She wants me to put her up for a few days.'

'Oh,' said Murray. 'Well, I can't advise you on that one I'm afraid. I've been married forty-nine years and I'm still cutting the lawn the wrong way, according to my wife, that is.' He chuckled. 'Do you think young Hadley is involved in these kidnappings and murders?'

'No, sir. I believe someone is trying to frame him. We can't ask him any questions. I think someone stole his handkerchief and his phone. The lad was always at the gym. It could have been someone there, or even someone here.'

'Well, you've always been a good judge of character, Jack. I can't deny that. I think he's innocent too.'

'What about Dublin? Shall I get ready?'

'I've booked my flight. I've got all the documents I need. I'm going in an hour.'

'I thought you wanted me to go, sir?'

'No, Jack. I think it's best you stay here and question that doctor when they find him. I've just got time to call at the hospital to see Hadley before my flight. I might have a bit more clout getting what we need from the consultant, being a Chief Inspector.'

'That's fine by me.' said Jack 'I'm up to my neck with things here and now my bloody ex-wife turns up.'

'You're banking on the suspect being at the clinic the same time as Amelia Stevens,' said Murray. 'I hope you're right about that, Jack. We could be barking up the wrong tree. The limp could have just been an attempt to disguise himself, to throw us off the scent, you might say.'

'I realise that, sir,' said Jack, 'but it's the only thing I have to link Amelia with the man who was seen at the library. If he is the one we're looking for he knew a lot about Amelia. He knew where to find her, or get in touch with her. She trusted him enough to get in the car with him.'

'Well, I hope you're right,' Murray rubbed his chest. 'I'd better get going or I'll miss the flight. I've arranged to speak with the consultant first thing tomorrow. It's the only day he'll be there, then he's off to America for a month. Did you know that lawns have a grain?'

'No sir.'

'Neither did I.'

*

Michael stirred, stretched his legs and opened his eyes. He looked at his watch. He'd slept for almost two hours. Catherine had been unconscious when he left her. It was time to finish the job and put her in the hole. He got up from the settee and fetched a hammer from the kitchen. He was about to go to her room when someone knocked on the door.

Steven stood on the step. 'Mark. You have to explain to me why you hit that young man. What's going on?'

'Come in. I want to tell you everything. You've been lost for so long, David, or shall I call you Steven?'

'I prefer Steven if you don't mind.'

They moved through the dark hallway of dingy, peeling gold flock wallpaper, broken wall light fittings and an oak floor littered with dust and dead leaves. 'Sorry about the mess. I haven't had time to renovate the place yet.' Michael opened the lounge door.

'I've been having weird dreams for a long time,' said Steven as he sat down on an old brown leather couch. 'Our childhood keeps coming back to me. I was confused at first. I'm remembering things much more clearly now. Father abused you, didn't he?'

'He did,' said Michael. 'What else do you remember?'

'It comes back in bits and pieces. I was at Green Fields orphanage. The night master was named John Thomas Naylor. Everyone called him Jonty. I was adopted by the Munroes when I was twelve. They told me I had an accident at the orphanage which delayed the adoption by three months. But I couldn't remember the past after the accident. I was fine for a while, then the nightmares began. They went away when I went through medical school and became a doctor. I'm working at Conley under Mr Douglas Darby. The nightmares returned about six months ago. I've been looking for you.' He took some papers from his coat pocket. 'Here are our birth certificates.'

Michael took the papers from him and glanced through them. 'Would you like some tea? Then I'll tell you everything.'

'Yes, I would. I've had nothing all day. I had to go somewhere quiet to think. Then everything started coming back to me. You don't know how thrilled I was to see you, Mark. My parents think I'm going camping in North Wales.'

Michael smiled. 'You can call me Michael. I left Mark behind a long time ago. I'll make us some tea then we can talk.'

Michael returned with a tray and put it on a small table next to the couch. He poured a cup and handed it to Steven. 'Drink up. Then I'll tell you what I've been doing since I left The Willows Children's Home.'

Steven took the cup and drank from it. 'I'm confused about things, Michael. The young man said he was a policeman. Why did you hit him like that? You might have killed him.'

'Can you imagine how I felt? I hadn't seen you for so long and he was there, trying to stop our meeting.'

'But he seemed to know you. How did he know you?'

'I work for the police. I'll show you my uniform. I found out he was involved in a major crime. He was trying to frame me for it.'

'You could have just arrested him.'

'I couldn't! He's too dangerous. He's already murdered someone,' Michael said angrily. 'And he was ruining my plans! If he'd spoken to you he would have known I was on to him.'

Steven put his empty cup back on the tray. 'How would he have known? We look the same. He must have thought I was you. God, I feel so lightheaded. I can't think straight. It must be lack of food.'

'I'm talking about revenge, Steven. It's been eating away at me for years. The people who hurt me must be punished.'

Steven slumped back in the chair. 'I feel really dizzy. What's happening?' His words had become slurred. 'What did you put in the tea?'

'Just a little something to make you sleep, brother. I haven't forgotten how you watched and laughed when father raped me. Do you think I would let you get away with it?' He stood up and leaned over Steven.

'But I... Mark! I didn't...'

'You were his snitch. You reported back to him!' He poked Steven's chest with long spidery fingers. 'Everything I said about him, everything I did! I wondered how he knew so much. Then I realised it was you!'

'Mark! Michael! You have to listen to me... I can't remember this...'

'Now it's payback time. You, dear brother, will get the blame for all this and I'll take your place. I was the cripple who they hid away, remember? They were ashamed of me. But you? Dear little David went to school. You became the doctor I wanted to be. They weren't ashamed of you, were they?' Michael lifted his arms in the air then slapped them down on his thighs. 'Oh, I am looking forward to being a real doctor! You wouldn't believe how happy I was to find out you'd done all of the work for me. Of course I'll have to kill you. But before I do, I'll have to break your leg to make it look like mine.' He laughed. 'You must become the cripple!'

'I'm… sor… ry… I… was scared he would… do… it to… me..'

'Shut up!' Michael shouted and picked up the hammer. 'You always were a snivelling coward! I tried to get rid of you in the fire but you got out.'

'I'm… sorry…' Steven slumped unconscious in the chair.

*

Michael went to Catherine's room. He had to finish her off and put her in the hole. When he opened the door to her room his mouth dropped open. Then he looked under the sink and screamed.

'No!'

*

Lily shook from head to toe. She could hear the baby crying faintly through the closed drawer. The Doctor screamed again. It was so loud she thought he was in the room with her. She sat on the bed rocking back and forth.

'Please God, don't let him torture her. I'm ready to die now, so take me, but let my baby live. Make her quiet, so that he won't hurt her. Please help me.'

A loud bang echoed round the house. The Doctor slammed the door of Catherine's room. 'Where are you? You bitch!' He screamed as he opened the back door and began to search round the outhouses and workshop. 'You won't get away! I'm coming for you, Catherine!'

*

'Can I have a word, sir?' Wallace was at Jack's door again.

'Come in,' said Jack. 'What is it?'

'Do you know the Prince Albert public house at Gall Heath?'

'Yes.'

'The landlord is Michael Brook. He came in just now with his daughter Emily to report a suspicious car lurking around by the shop where she works last week. She only told him about it today. Here's the plate number. She didn't know the make of the car, she said it was black and quite big. Do you think it might be that Audi we're looking for?'

'Could well be, Wallace. Put the number out and get a patrol car to keep a watch on the shop. And give Claude Benson a call. See if he recognises the number.'

'Yes, sir. Another thing is she has long blond hair and blue eyes, like the other victims.'

'It might be our man looking for another girl and that could mean he's going to kill again. We know from the note on the arrow that Catherine has displeased him in some way. Let me know when Sergeant Poole gets back from Bordley.'

'Yes, sir.' Wallace closed the door as he left.

The phone rang. 'Jack Riley.'

'Jack.'

'Gwen? Is everything ok?'

'I'm sorry, Jack.'

'What for?'

'Oh, just the way I am with you. I need to tell you something, but not over the phone.'

'It's okay. I understand. It's wrong of me to assume you would want to go out with me again. I'm sorry for asking. Three times.'

'It's not about that, Jack. Can you come round tonight?'

'I'll do my best, Gwen. I'm waiting to interview someone at the minute. As soon as I'm done I'll ring you if it's not too late. You're all right, aren't you? It's nothing urgent?'

'Well, it is important. Try to come, Jack.'

'I'll get someone to cover for me. I'll be there. Don't worry.'

Jack was still at his desk when Sergeant Poole came back from Bordley.

'Sir, I can't find this Doctor Munroe anywhere. I've been to his house again. His father said he left for his holiday early this morning. Conley General confirmed he's on leave. I've been there twice now.'

'You've got his car registration. Put it out to all units.'

'Yes, sir.'

DS Morgan appeared in the doorway. 'No luck with the doctor then?'

'Not yet. We're looking at CCTV in and around the library and down to the traffic lights towards Tipley to see if we can see which way he left town.'

'It'll take forever. Do you know how much traffic goes along that road?'

'Yes, but we only need to look in an hour time frame, don't we? Say half hour before the time in Hadley's notebook and half hour after.' Jack moved to go out. 'I'm sorry about last night.'

'Well, I suppose I overreacted.' DS Morgan followed him to the computer room. 'It's because of all the shit I had before when I got the job. Sorry, Jack. I didn't mean Marty Feldman either.' she laughed. 'In fact you remind me of a younger Brendan Coyle.'

Jack smiled and put his arm round her shoulder. 'Let's just forget the whole thing, shall we? Who the hell is Brendan Coyle, anyway?'

'You haven't watched Downton Abbey?'

'No, but I've heard of it. He must be good looking then?'

'Watch it and judge for yourself,' DS Morgan smiled. 'I hope Hadley's going to be ok. He's the only one who can tell us what happened.'

'Apart from the attacker,' said Jack. 'And I don't think he'll be in any hurry to tell us. Have you found out anything else about the Cartwrights?'

'That's exactly why I'm here. Mrs Cartwright's neighbour told me there was a grandson who used to stay with her. So I did a bit of digging at the register office and records with social services. I wanted to know what happened to the grandson because the grandmother obviously didn't have him. There wasn't a grandson, there were two. Identical twins. Mark and David. They were ten years old when their parents died and they were almost twelve when their grandmother died. If they were in care it's doubtful they could have had anything to do with the grandmother's death. But one of them was put in Green Leaves Children's Home, just two miles from the grandmother's house.'

'What about the other one?'

'He went to a home for disturbed children, somewhere in Kent, for twelve months then got transferred to The Willows Children's Home, which is on the main road towards Barton. About ten miles from here. I'm trying to track them down. They would be around twenty-four or twenty-five now. The same age group as the killer.'

'Did you find anything on Bennett?'

'Well that's something else. I had to go back a long way. Twenty-five years ago, he was accused of touching a young girl on a train. The train was crowded. His solicitor argued that he was pushed up close to her and it was accidental touching. He was found not guilty and the case was dismissed.'

'Nothing since then?'

'No. He got married two years later and took up the post at Saint Edmunds.'

'What about his car?'

'It's a ten-year-old silver Vauxhall Nova.'

'You've been busy and you've done well, Sandy. Thank you. I have to go and see Gwen. Is there any chance you can hang on here in case Sergeant Poole locates Doctor Munroe? I'd rather you interview him.'

'Yes, I'll stay here a while.'

Chapter Thirty-Four

'I must keep moving,' Catherine murmured to herself as she crawled through the long grass. 'I must keep moving.'

It had taken a long time to get out of the hole. She'd fallen back so many times she almost gave up. Her knees, feet and hands were caked with soil and blood and her wrist had swollen to the size of a golf ball. She sat down to take a breath. She thought about her father who had so cruelly used her mother's illness to do wicked things to her. She was going to tell her mother everything if she made it home. She had to. She couldn't live this lie any longer. There would be no more fear, no more lies. Not after this.

She looked across the field towards a hedge and wondered if there was a road on the other side. It seemed a long way off. To her left the field seemed to stretch for miles, with no hedge in sight. The view to her right was the same, except there were a few trees dotted around. She reasoned that the Doctor would expect her to go straight across the field towards the hedge. She turned right and headed towards the trees.

*

Gwen opened the door and beckoned Jack to the lounge. 'Thanks for coming,' she said as they sat down.

Jack looked at her. Her eyes were red, as if she'd been crying. 'What's up, Gwen?'

'I need to tell you something, Jack. I don't know how to do it.'

'If it's about Stella…'

'No, Jack it's not that.'

'You know me well enough to tell me anything. Come on. What is it?'

'It's about my son, William.'

'What's he done?'

'He hasn't done anything. It's me. I've lied to him.'

'We all tell our kids white lies. It's not the end of the world.'

'I've lied to you too, Jack. Do you want a drink before I tell you?'

'You're worrying me now. I think I'd better. I'll have a whiskey if you have some.'

'I have some,' she said and went to the kitchen.

'Where's William anyway? I thought you said he was home for the summer.' Jack called after her.

She came back in the room with two glasses of whiskey and handed one to Jack.

'We had a bit of an argument earlier. He's gone out. He went on his motorcycle. I hope he doesn't do anything silly, Jack,' she started to cry.

Jack jumped out of the chair, took the drinks from her and put them on the table.

'Come and sit down. Tell me what's wrong.'

'I've told him the truth, Jack.'

'The truth about what?'

'You're his father, Jack. I'm so sorry for not telling you.'

Jack felt as if the air had been squeezed from his lungs. He covered his eyes with his fingertips and took a deep breath. 'Gwen, I can't deal with this right now. There's too much going on at the minute.'

Chapter Thirty-Five

Jack left Gwen's house in a daze. He got in his car and drove home. He couldn't come to terms with what she'd told him, too much to take in. There were questions he wanted to ask, but he was numb.

William was his son and Gwen had kept it from him for almost twenty years. He didn't know how to feel about it. He thought back to their days at university. She had suddenly wanted to change her course, to leave the town altogether and start a new career. He was gutted at the time. Then Susan told him she was pregnant with his child. He'd cheated on Gwen with her. Once. But once was all it needed to ruin his life. He wondered if Gwen had known at the time and had made her decision because of it. He knew he would have to talk to her. He needed some answers.

He sat down and poured a glass of whiskey. His head spun with thoughts of Lily and Susan, back to add more stress to his life. Now Gwen. Another bombshell. He didn't know what to do next.

His phone rang. 'Sandy. Sorry I couldn't get back. Has Poole located Doctor Munroe yet?'

'No. No sign of him, Jack. You sound a bit winded. Have you been running?'

'No, everything's fine,' Jack's voice cracked.

'Are you sure? Is Gwen okay?'

'Sandy I can't talk at the moment. I'll be back in soon.' Jack pressed the call off.

*

Catherine stopped to get her breath. It must have been an hour since she'd started to walk this way.

'Catherine! You won't escape! I'm coming for you!'

She crouched down, afraid to move or even breathe. A tree rustled and her heart missed a beat. 'He can see me,' she murmured. 'Oh my god!' A squirrel ran across her foot, she retracted it quickly. The long grass around her swished and swayed in the breeze. She was sure he was close by. She lay still for a few more minutes. Then she moved. She began to crawl. Slowly. She could see a hedge a few yards in front of her and wondered if there was another field beyond it or a road. She made her way towards the thicket and prayed there would be a gap that she could crawl through.

Michael had gone halfway across the field when he realised there was no bent grass, or any kind of trail where someone could have walked. The bitch had gone left or right across the field and he didn't have time to look both ways. He decided right, and ran as fast as he could.

In the distance he could see movement in the long grass. She was heading towards a thicket and beyond that a road. He stopped to gauge how far she was from the road.

He had to stop her, he couldn't let her get away now, his plans would all be ruined.

*

Jack poured his second whiskey. His mobile phone had been in his hand for half an hour as he debated whether or not to call Gwen. He'd left her crying in the hallway of her house and now he felt guilty. He was also worried about William. What a mess he'd made of his life. Not one relationship in his life had been happy or successful.

His mother hated him. Susan had given up on him. He'd lost his precious Lily. And Gwen. What had he done to her? He scrolled to her number and pressed 'call'.

She picked up on the third ring. 'Hello, Jack.' Her voice sounded hoarse.

'We need to talk, Gwen. I'm sorry I left like that. Can I come back over there?'

'Yes. Jack I need you here. He's not back yet. I'm so worried about him.'

'I'm on my way.'

*

Catherine heard the swish of his clothes as he ran through the grass. He was getting closer. She tried to run but her legs felt as if heavy weights had been attached to them. She had to stop and hide.

'Where are you, Catherine? He called in a sing-song voice.

She pushed her way through brambles and cut her

hands and face on thorns and twigs. Then she fell in a ditch. He stopped a foot away from the bramble hedge and walked slowly up and down. She was afraid to breathe. If he stepped back he would fall into the ditch beside her.

The bitch had escaped. He knew he had to get back to the house and finish things there, then go. If she'd been picked up by a passing motorist the police would be here within minutes. He ran back to the house.

Chapter Thirty-Six

Lily could hear the Doctor as he shouted and slammed doors. Hope drained from her heart. He was going to kill her. Catherine had escaped and he'd been out searching for her. He sounded raving mad as he stormed around the house.

The baby had been quiet for a long time. She wondered if she had died in the drawer. Perhaps it would be the best thing to happen to her. Better than being murdered by a madman. She thought of her father. He hadn't come to save her. She couldn't blame him. She didn't want to die with ill feelings about her beloved daddy.

He was the one person who had loved her throughout her childhood, given her all he could, made her smile, made her happy.

'I love you, Daddy,' she whispered. She fetched the baby from the drawer and laid on the bed with her. 'The only thing I can do for you now is to give you a name and hold you in my arms. Hello, Daisy.'

*

Steven was still lying where he'd left him on the couch. He had to work fast. He began to undress him. He dressed Steven in his work uniform, put his driving license in his coat pocket and stuffed a handkerchief from his own pocket into Steven's trouser pocket. Then he carried him up to the attic and dropped him on the floor. He went back downstairs to get the sledgehammer.

*

Gwen opened the door and Jack followed her into the lounge. She sat down and put her head in her hands. 'Jack, I'm sorry.'

'It's a bit of a shock. Perhaps you'd like to tell me the whole story,' he sat next to her.

'You hurt me, Jack. I just wanted to get away from the situation.'

'You broke my heart,' said Jack.

Gwen turned quickly. 'Oh! You didn't break mine then? I didn't go off with someone else!'

'You went off with Jon! You bloody married him!'

'You went off with Susan. I never went with Jon behind your back. Don't you realise how much you hurt me?'

'Yes,' Jack admitted with tears in his eyes. 'It was my fault. I've made a big mess of my life.'

'It was confusing for me at the time, so I thought I'd better leave. I knew about Susan, you see. That's what made me go.'

'You knew I'd had a one night stand with her?' said Jack.

'She didn't put it like that. She said you were dating and she was pregnant.'

'It was a one night stand and I've regretted it all my life, except for Lily. I thought you didn't want to be with me anymore when you left, so I married her because of the baby.'

'She told me you were getting married, Jack. I had to go, I was dead inside.'

Jack moved closer and put his arm around her. 'I'm sorry Gwen. I didn't ask her to marry me until after you'd gone. If I'd known about William I wouldn't have married her at all.'

'Oh, Jack, what a mess we've made!'

'She's back in England. She phoned and asked me to put her up for a few days. I said no. I don't want her in my life, Gwen. You can't imagine how much I regret I have over losing you.'

'I think I can. I'm really worried about William though. In his eyes Jon was his father. When I told him earlier he was very angry.'

'Well, it's a shock for him. He's entitled to be angry. I've had all that shit myself from my mother. Don't worry. We'll face this together. Does he have a mobile phone?'

'It's there on the table, he didn't take it with him. He's going to hate me for this Jack, I know he is.'

'Initially, maybe. After a while the good parts come back. The days spent baking with you, or going to the park, the bruised knees you kissed better.'

'Jack, you're making me cry.'

'Well after what my mother did, I hated her for a while. But for the life she gave me, the sacrifices she made for me, I love her with all my heart. Even though she might not know it. And William will always love you, no matter what. Trust me. He will forgive you.'

'Can you forgive me, Jack?'

'Well I've been deprived of sharing my son's life. I've missed so much of him growing up.'

'I know. I'm so sorry, Jack.'

'It's a lot to take in at the moment. I need to find Lily. Then maybe we can try to sort out everything else.'

*

Catherine found a gap in the hedgerow and scrambled through it. She found herself on a grass verge. There was a road. She crawled towards the road and stood up.

Headlights were coming towards her. She put her hands up and waved. Surely the driver would see her. She dropped to the ground as the car swerved to avoid her and stopped a few yards down the road. She was suddenly filled with horror. What if this was the Doctor? He had probably come to look for her. She had to get up, she had to run, but before she could move the driver was out of the car and running towards her.

'What are you doing in the middle of the road? You could have been killed.'

'Help me, please! I'm Catherine Bennett. I've escaped from my kidnapper. I need to see Inspector

Jack Riley. His daughter Lily is still alive.'

'Come on,' said the young man, as he helped her to stand. 'You're in no fit state to see anyone. You need to go to hospital.'

*

'I'll get the patrol cars to keep an eye out for William,' said Jack and took his phone from his pocket. He was just about to ring the station when it rang. 'Riley here.'

'Sir, this is Sergeant Poole. I have a young man on the other line who says he's taken Catherine Bennett to hospital. He found her in the road on his way to Tipley. She told him Lily is still alive. She collapsed before she could tell him where she'd been kept. He said he can show us where he found her. Shall I send Jones and a couple of the other lads with him, sir?'

'You go with them. Send everyone you can round up. We don't know what we're dealing with. I'm coming to meet you.' Jack put his phone in his pocket. 'I have to go, Gwen. Catherine Bennett has been found, she's at the hospital. She says Lily is alive. I'll call about William on the way to meet them. Don't worry, I'm sure he'll be fine.'

Chapter Thirty-Seven

Steven was coming round when he got back to the attic.

'Well brother, it looks like my wishes are coming true.' He dropped the sledgehammer on the floor. 'You are going to take my place now and I'll take yours. For all the crimes you committed you're going to jump from the attic and kill yourself but first there's the little matter of your leg. It's got to match mine you see.' He laughed.

'Please, Mark! Please don't kill me!' Steven begged. 'I was a child. I laughed to protect myself from him! I'm a different person now. I'm sorry! Before I had my accident at the orphanage, I sneaked out and killed our grandmother. I lost my memory after I fell out of the tree, but I'm remembering it all now. I did it for us, Mark. She didn't want us.'

'She didn't want you! I've told you, I'm not Mark anymore! You did it for you, brother! Not me! You were a selfish brat! I never went to school until I went to the orphanage. I was kept away from normal people until I was put away. They looked on me as a freak! And so did you! You never cared what he did to me! You told tales to him so that he'd punish me. You were evil! Now you're going to pay!' He lifted the sledgehammer to shoulder height and was about to swing it when Steven suddenly jumped up and dived at him.

Michael dropped the hammer and fell backwards to the floor. Steven jumped on top of him. They fought frantically as each tried to prevent the other from getting to the hammer. He gripped his brother's hair and banged his head against a large wooden beam three or four times. Steven stopped struggling. He was out. Michael stood up and grabbed the hammer. He lifted it shoulder high and heard bones crack as he landed a forceful blow to his brother's left knee. Eight more times he swung the hammer until he was satisfied the lower leg, thigh, knee and ankle were shattered. He gave the other leg a few hard blows, then dragged the lifeless body across the room, lifted it on to the window ledge, opened the window and let it fall feet first.

'Goodbye Michael! 'Hello Steven!' he laughed.

There wasn't much blood to clean up, it hadn't had time to seep through Steven's trousers. It would look like a suicide to the police. When he realised Catherine had escaped he knew the game was up. This was his only way out.

Everything was ready for him to go. He had the keys to the house at Bordley and debated whether to call there or not. Would it help his case if he turned up there oblivious to the fact that everyone was looking for him? Where could he say he'd been all this time since Hadley had been attacked? He had no alibi. He had to go.

Steven's holdall was in his car. He went through it and found some jeans and a sweater and put them on.

He had to go now. He would use this week to read and study the job his brother did at the hospital, then he would take his place there. Who would know? They were identical twins. He headed out to Wales. There would be no newspapers or television where he was going and his mobile phone would be switched off. Hadley was in a coma with brain damage. There wasn't much chance he'd ever recover.

*

As Jack raced towards Tipley, DS Jones called to tell him they were at Tipley Manor House, they'd found the two cars used to kidnap the girls in a field behind the property and were getting ready to go in. He was less than a mile away and put his foot down.

DS Jones, four constables and Sergeant Poole were waiting by the front door.

'Let's do it!' shouted Jack as he jumped out of the car. 'My daughter's in there with that maniac!'

Jones and Poole rammed their bodies in to the door and it swung open. The hallway was dark and smelled of damp. Towards the back of the house was a hallway with doors on either side. Jack pushed open every door he passed. Then he came to a room that was painted white. The door was half open and there were three bolts on the outside. He looked round. It was empty, but a single metal framed bed looked as if it had been slept in. Other bedclothes were draped over a radiator. A cupboard under the sink was open and he could see a large hole in the wall. There was blood on the bed and drips across the floor that stopped at the sink. The strong smell of carbolic soap filled the room.

'This must be the room Catherine escaped from,' he said to the constable at his side. 'Don't touch anything.'

The next door was bolted from the outside. Three bolts. Jack shook as he slid the across and opened the door. Someone was on the bed, curled in a ball, not moving.

'Lily?' Jack's voice croaked. 'Lily?'

The girl looked up. Her face was as white as a sheet, her hair lank and long, hung around her face. Her eyes were red.

'My daddy! Oh my daddy!' she cried.

Jack strode across the room and took her in his arms.

Jones came in the room. 'Sir, there's a body at the back of the house. It looks like Mackenzie.'

Sergeant Poole appeared in the doorway. 'He's still alive! Call an ambulance!'

'Shall I put him out of his misery?' DS Jones asked. 'He's a fucking animal!'

'Keep your hands off him, Jones,' said Jack. 'I don't want you in any trouble.'

Chapter Thirty-Eight

Two ambulances and a forensic team were parked on the drive of Tipley Manor. Crime scene tape was stretched across the gates and Sergeant Poole stood just inside to check everyone who arrived.

Jack sat inside one of the ambulances and watched intently as medics tended to Lily and her baby. Lily, grey faced, cried into Jack's shoulder when one of the medics said the baby was dehydrated and had a temperature.

'Don't worry,' said Jack as he patted her back. 'She'll be okay.'

DS Jones looked in through the open door. 'I'm glad we found her, sir,' his voice cracked. 'That date with Gwen. All she did was talk about you. I'm sorry for the grief, I was a bit peeved she didn't fancy me.'

'Stop putting that grease on your hair,' said Jack. 'You might have more luck with the ladies.' DS Jones smiled and put his hand up.

In the other ambulance medics battled to stabilise Mackenzie's heart beat before they took him to hospital. Leg bones protruded through his trousers and he was covered in blood.

Gwen, wearing her white overalls, head cap, boots and gloves was going in and out of the house taking samples. She saw Jack in the ambulance and went to speak to him.

'How's she doing?'

'She's doing okay. Have you found anything interesting in there?'

'Yes. I found a baby upstairs. A boy. It's possible he's Amelia's baby. He has some kind of metal brace attached to his legs. He's in a bad way. We need to get him to hospital as soon as possible.'

'Did you hear it was Mackenzie?'

'Yes, but I've never met him.'

'He's a PCSO. He's been working at the station about eight weeks. Has William turned up?'

'Yes. He's quiet, but was back before I came out here. I'll speak to you later.'

'We're ready, Inspector,' said one of the ambulance crew. 'Will you be coming along with us?'

'I most certainly will,' said Jack. ' I'm not letting my girl out of my sight. Let's go!'

Sunday morning

Jack had stepped outside Lily's hospital room to take a call from Murray.

'Jack!'

'Yes, I'm here, sir!'

'There's no-one by the name of Cartwright on the consultant's records. But Mackenzie's name's on the list, Jack! His treatment lasted around three years.'

'We have him, sir! He tried to top himself when Catherine Bennett escaped. It looks like he jumped from an attic window. He wasn't killed in the fall. He's in intensive care.'

'Let's hope he lives. He needs to suffer after what he's done to those girls and Miss Baker. How is Lily?'

'She's very weak. She's had a baby who's fighting for her life at the minute and she won't move away from her.'

'God, Jack! She must have gone through hell. Stay with her. Don't worry about anything else. Have you traced the doctor who was on Broad Street at the time Hadley was attacked?'

'No, sir.'

'Maybe he didn't see anything. It seems to me that Mackenzie attacked Hadley because he was on to him.'

'Maybe. I don't know. I think we should still question the doctor when we find him.'

'I'll be back late. I'll see you tomorrow.'

'Yes, okay, sir.' As soon as Jack put the phone in his pocket it rang again.

'Jack. It's Ted. The doc said I can come back to work.'

'That's great, Ted! We certainly need you here. Has anyone told you we have the killer? It was Mackenzie.'

'No! One of our own! What about Lily? Is she safe?'

'She's at the hospital. She's had a baby, Ted.'

'Tell her I'll come to see her. My god, I'm so relieved she's okay.'

'There's a lot more to tell you, Ted, but I'm still at the hospital. I'll bring you up to date tomorrow.'

'Fine. I'll see you in the morning. Jack, did you say it was Mackenzie? He has a double who works at Conley Hospital. I've been trying to think where I'd seen the young doctor before. It was at the station. Mackenzie has a twin.'

'What?'

'The young doctor who examined me. He's the spit of Mackenzie, Jack.'

'Doctor Munroe?'

'Yes, that's him.'

'Mackenzie changed his name. They must be the Cartwright twins.'

Chapter Thirty-Nine

One week later

Jack and DS Morgan were in his office drinking coffee.

'So Mark Cartwright changed his name to Michael Mackenzie when he was having his ops in Dublin and Steven Munroe is his twin brother, David, who was adopted?'

'Yes. I traced the adoption for David. I also found the deed poll for Mark, along with their birth certificates. Their father was the renowned plastic surgeon, Mr Matthew Cartwright, and Tipley Manor was their country home.' DS Morgan put a folder on the desk. 'It's all in here.'

Jack picked the folder up and opened it. 'Mackenzie was only a part timer. We didn't see much of him. He wasn't at any crime scenes but he was here on the Saturday after Catherine was abducted. He also worked part time for Fast Bytes Technology and had glowing references from his tutors in Dublin, where he gained a first class degree in computer technology.

He must have messed with the computers. He tried to frame Hadley because he knew Catherine liked the lad and it would lead us in the wrong direction. You've worked hard on this case, Sandy. You've done really well.' Jack sipped his coffee. 'I'm going to recommend you for promotion and I hope you can stay with us. You're doing a better job than me.'

'I haven't heard from Superintendent Middleton yet. He knows I want to stay here. I wouldn't have done any of it without you, Jack. You pointed me to the Cartwright family. You insisted on finding that car. You gave me the directions to follow. Don't you dare put yourself down! You're a brilliant copper!'

'Thanks, but you deserve a lot of credit for what you've done.'

'How are the girls?'

'Lily and the baby are doing well. So is Catherine. They're staying at my mother's at the moment. Her father's in custody for the abuse he put her through and her mother's in hospital. She's had a breakdown. Amelia's baby is still critical. The grandparents are at his bedside.'

'The poor lad. I can't imagined how he's suffered.'

'I've put my flats up for sale. It's too upsetting to be there now Stella has gone. We can't stay there. Lily wants a garden for the baby.' Jack looked at the folder again. 'Miss Judy Grey. Councillor Lloyd's maiden name.'

'Yes, she was one of the people who decided Mark Cartwright needed to be locked away in that home for disturbed children at Barton. Along with the committee chairman, Mr Chapman.'

'Mackenzie's still in a coma,' said Jack.

'What about David Cartwright, I mean Doctor Steven Munroe? He's due back from holiday, isn't he?' Sandy sipped her coffee.

'His parents know we want to talk to him. I'm surprised he hasn't seen the appeals for him to come forward or that no-one has seen him anywhere.'

'We need to talk to him, Jack. What about the grandmother's death? Was it suicide or murder?'

'Murray thinks he's got nothing to do with what his brother's done. Or with the grandmother's death, even though he was in Green Fields at the time. He thinks the old woman killed herself because of her son's death.'

'There was another death at Green Fields around the same time the grandmother died. John Thomas Naylor, one of the night staff was found in the laundry room with a plastic bag on his head and a broom handle so far up his backside it touched his tonsils.'

'I remember that. He was a drug user. He was off his head, according to the coroner's report. I think it was assumed he was trying to get some kind of sexual high from asphyxiation while using the broomstick. But he passed out and fell on the broom.'

'My god! It's amazing what some people get up to.' Sandy stood up and moved to the door.

'Isn't it just?'

*

Doctor Steven Munroe packed his tent in the boot of his car and headed back to the West Midlands. He hadn't had a decent meal for a week and stopped at a country pub to enjoy a full English breakfast. Steven Munroe was a junior doctor in the Dermatology Department at Conley General Hospital studying under Mr Douglas Darby. He'd spent the week studying various skin diseases he might encounter in his work at the hospital. He was apprehensive about going there, but his biggest fear was convincing his brother's adoptive parents that he was the Steven they knew. That morning he'd trimmed his beard and combed his hair with a parting on the right side, just like Steven. He wore Steven's Nike trainers, with an added sole on the left one, his track suit and a pair of spectacles with plain glass. 'Who looks at a man's shoes?' he said in his Morgan Freeman voice from *The Shawshank Redemption.*

He shook his doubts aside. 'I am Doctor Steven Munroe,' he said. 'No-one will think otherwise. He pulled up outside the house at Bordsley. 'Well here goes,' he smiled to himself. The door opened before he could get out of the car and Mr Munroe stood on the step and waved to him.

Mrs Munroe put a tray on the table and began to pour tea into three cups.

'It's good to have you back, son,' said Mr Munroe as he pulled out a chair and sat next to his son. 'The police have been here after you. They want you to go to the station to help them with an attack on a police officer. What were you doing in Dudstone, son?'

'Father, I'm so sorry I went there. I went to meet my brother but he didn't turn up so I went on my camping trip. You don't know how much I regret looking for him.'

'Don't fret about it, Stevie. I only want to know where you were.'

'Well. When he didn't turn up I was initially disappointed. I drove around for a while. Then I drove to Wales.'

'I knew you had nothing to do with it, son. That's what I told them.' Mr Munroe put an arm round his shoulder. 'Don't worry lad.'

'I won't. All I want is to be here with you and carry on with my work at Conley. And I'm through with looking for my brother. I don't want anything to do with him. If he comes here, you must turn him away.'

Mr Munroe looked at his wife, then back to his son. 'You haven't heard then?'

'Heard what? I've been in the Welsh mountains, Father, living on beans and soup. I haven't seen anyone, except for the odd walker on the mountains.'

'Your brother is a murderer. He's killed people, he's kidnapped girls. It's been all over the papers and television.'

'He did what? He killed people?'

'Yes, son. You're better off not knowing him.'

'Oh my god! What kind of a family have I come from?'

'According to the papers he's still in a coma.'

Steven's right eye began to twitch . He lifted his hand to cover it. 'What... happened... to him?' he stammered.

'Don't get upset about it, lad. He's not worth crying over. He jumped from a window, tried to kill himself.'

'But... he... should have died,' said Steven. 'He should have died.'

Chapter Forty

'There's plenty of evidence to convict Mackenzie of the abductions and murders,' said Jack.

'I heard they amputated his left leg and he's shown signs of waking from the coma.' Sandy sat down at Jack's desk.

'He should have died,' said Jack. 'I could have easily killed him. We found the bow he used to kill Councillor Lloyd and items of clothing belonging to Lily, Catherine and Amelia. Hadley's phone was there too. He's just a sick bastard. He had a wedding dress and a suit ready to marry someone. Whichever one he chose.'

'He chose all of them, but they didn't come up to his expectations of what a wife should be like.'

'Catherine and Lily said he called them Rebecca. Is there anyone of that name linked to the Cartwright family?'

'Not that I know of.'

'I might give Claude Benson a call. He seemed to

know all about them.'

'We don't really need to know anymore, Jack. We have him and we have the evidence.'

There was a knock on the door and DS Jones came in. 'Doctor Steven Munroe's here. Where shall I put him?'

'Room one,' said Jack. 'Get a note book, Sandy.'

Doctor Steven Munroe sat opposite Jack and DS Morgan. The room seemed chilly for the time of year. August was usually warmer. He was dressed in a smart grey suit, white shirt and pale blue tie. Jack thought the tie matched the colour of his eyes, which were fixed on the notebook in front of DS Morgan.

'Thank you for coming in Doctor Munroe,' said Jack. 'I'm Detective Inspector Riley and this is my colleague, Detective Sergeant Morgan. We have to clear up an issue regarding the attack on one of our officers, Constable Hadley on the evening of the twenty-fifth of July. Constable Hadley had recorded seeing your car parked on Broad Street around the time he was attacked. Can I ask you what you were doing in the area?'

'I was waiting for my brother, Inspector.'

'What is your brother's name?'

'Well his birth name is Mark Cartwright, but I've learned from my father that he's now called Michael Mackenzie.'

'What was the purpose of your meeting?'

'We hadn't seen each other since we were ten years old. Our parents died in a fire and we were put in different orphanages. I was very excited about meeting him.'

'How did you get in touch with him after all that time?'

'He left a note on my car at the hospital where I work,' he sighed. 'Inspector I had a bad accident some years ago which impaired my memory. I didn't recall having a brother until recently. At the time I had the accident the doctors said my memory could return or it may never return. I've been very happy with my adoptive parents, but obviously I was delighted to find I had a brother. My memory of the past has been coming back the last few weeks. I remembered my brother. I wanted to meet him, but he never showed up.'

'You didn't see another car on Broad Street while you were there?'

'No.'

'Did Constable Hadley speak to you?'

'No. I didn't see or speak with anyone, Inspector. My brother didn't turn up, so I left. I was rather disappointed.'

'Constable Hadley had written your car registration and the time he saw you in his note book. Are you absolutely sure you didn't see him?'

'I didn't see him. I must have driven off before he got out of his car, Inspector. The only car I did see was a small red one which overtook me before I passed the library.'

'Can you recall the make of the car?'

'I didn't really take much notice. It was travelling quite fast. I just saw this flash of red go by. I think it might have been a Ford Focus.'

'Well, I think that's all we need to ask you, Doctor Munroe. Thank you again for coming in.' Jack stood up and opened the door for the doctor. 'Oh, one more thing doctor. Does the name Rebecca mean anything to you?'

'Why… no… should it?'

'Not to worry. It doesn't really matter now.'

'I'm sorry I couldn't come sooner, but I was camped halfway up a mountain in Wales. I'm doing research on a new treatment for skin cancer.'

'Well, what do you make of him?' Jack asked after the doctor had left.

'He seems quite a pleasant young man,' said Sandy.

'I didn't mention that Hadley was in a car.'

'Perhaps he assumed it. You did ask if he'd seen any cars. Mackenzie has a red Ford Focus.'

'He actually said he must have driven off before Hadley got out of his car. How did he know Hadley was in a car if he didn't see one?'

'What are you looking for, Jack? We have our man. I think it was just a term of speech. He assumed Hadley was in a car. That's not saying he saw it.'

'My mind's in overdrive again. Everyone's guilty. Forget it.'

'I'd like to go and have a look round Tipley Manor now if you don't mind.'

'The team's still in. What are you looking for?'

'I'd like to see where the girls were kept. It helps to

build a better picture of what made this man tick. I'm just curious.'

'Help yourself. But don't get in Gwen's way. She's like a bomb ready to go off when she's working. She thinks she's found hidden treasure when she gets a sample.'

Jack laughed. 'But she's bloody good at her job!'

'I've heard she found a human bone under the operating table.'

'What? She hasn't told me about it. But she hasn't spoken to me for a few days.'

'She's busy at her treasure trove. I'll go and see what she's up to.'

'Fine. I'll see you later. Murray's coming in to see me. When I told him about the ring he said no-one could be exactly sure that Lily was wearing it when she was taken, so it couldn't be used as a link to the other cases.'

'Well, he obviously didn't want you to be in any trouble. I'll see you later.'

Jack picked up the phone when Sandy left and rang the scrap yard.

Claude Benson answered. 'Benson's Scrap Merchant.'

'Claude. It's Jack Riley here. I'd like to hear a bit of gossip.'

'What is it you want to know, Jack?'

'In connection with the Cartwrights. Did you know of anyone named Rebecca?'

'Only one girl by that name who had anything to do with them. She was nanny to his son for a few years. Rebecca Rawlings.'

'Any idea where she might be now, Claude?'

'She used to live in Segmore years ago. I'm not sure if she's still there. To be honest I think she moved away after she left the Cartwright's employment.'

'Thanks, Claude.'

'Matthew Cartwright had a half-sister, Jack. Nobody knew about her. I told you his father shagged anything that moved. He had her with that young receptionist who used to work for me. Her name was Eva Tyler.'

'Well, I'm not looking for anyone else in connection with the crimes that Mark Cartwright committed. I was just curious. My daughter said he used to call her Rebecca.'

'I know he's done some dreadful things, but you got to wonder what kind of a miserable life he had. Hardly anyone knew he existed. I thought there was only one lad living in the house that was burnt down. He used to come with his father to my garage at Bordley.'

'He's locked up now. Thanks Claude.'

Jack's phone was ringing when he went back in his office after his meeting with Murray. 'Hello, Jack Riley here.'

'It's me, Sandy. Are you doing anything at the moment?'

'No. What is it?'

'My god, Jack, you won't believe this! You have to see it to believe it. The walk-in freezer is full of body parts. Arms, legs, torsos with skin hanging off. It's like Frankenstein's laboratory in there. Jars of blood and eyeballs… it looks like it all rotted, then the electric was put back on and froze it again.'

'Shut up, Sandy!'

'Oh, sorry, Jack. I forgot about your stomach.'

'Is Gwen there?'

'She popped back to the lab with some hair and bone samples. She couldn't wait to get started on them.'

'I'll be there in fifteen minutes and you can show me all this sick stuff you're raving about.'

*

Sandy was waiting outside Tipley Manor when Jack arrived. 'You need to see the cellar, Jack. Have you been down here before?'

'No.'

'Well there's three huge rooms stretching the length and breadth of the entire manor. A wine cellar, a laundry and an operating theatre. There's a walk-in freezer in the operating room. That's where the body parts are.'

'What gave you the idea to look here?'

'The cleaner who worked for the Cartwrights, Mrs Cole. She went missing and her body was never found. Also Mr Matthew Cartwright was one of the visiting lecturers at Larchester University during the nineteen-nineties.'

'The Lost Girls?'

'Yes.'

'You think they're here?'

'I think they died here, Jack.'

Chapter Forty-One

During the next two days reporters and television crews camped outside Tipley Manor House, some occasionally pushing forward to try to get photographs of or statements from whoever went in or out. Every daily newspaper carried the story of the Lost Girls of Larchester. It would take months to determine how many girls had been murdered in the house of horror. Teams of forensic pathologists had already collected hundreds of bones and body parts.

Jack Riley was in his office reading one of the news reports when Murray came in.

'Good morning, sir.'

'Aren't you sick of reading about it, Jack?' Murray asked when he noticed the newspaper.

'There's a knot in my stomach,' said Jack. 'And a doubt in my mind.'

'Doubt? What about?'

'Mackenzie's awake. He doesn't know who he is or where he comes from. The nurses who look after him say he's mild natured and quietly spoken.'

'He's had a bad knock on the head. But my theory is he's trying to fool people in to believing he's no longer a threat to anyone. Forget about him. He's where he should be. The case is closed.' Murray stood up and went to the door. 'I'm retiring at Christmas, Jack. I want you to put in for my job.'

'I don't think I'm ready for it, sir.'

'Of course you are. I'm going to recommend you anyway. I want you to have a month off. Take a rest. Be with your little girl while she heals. Will you do that?'

'I'll take a month off. Starting next week.'

'Okay, that's settled.'

'Do you know what happened to Mackenzie's leg?'

'It went in the incinerator as far as I know. Why?'

'Did anyone look at it?'

'Look at it? They had to scoop it up on a shovel, so I was told. They only just managed to save the other one. Of course that left leg was already weakened from all the operations he'd had. What are you getting at?'

'What if we have the wrong one at the hospital?'

'Jack, your mind's in overdrive again. That's why I want you to have a month off. Let it go!'

'Yes, you're right. I'll forget about it. Who knows about your retirement? I don't want to say anything I shouldn't.'

'No-one at the moment. I'll tell everyone on Monday.'

'Your stomach seems better.'

'I'm taking a new pill. It's bloody marvellous. No more acid reflux.'

There was a knock on the door.

'Come in!' Murray called.

DS. Bateman stood in the doorway behind Murray. 'Excuse me, sir. There's a young lady here. She wants to see DI Riley.'

'Who is it, Ted?' Jack asked.

'She said her name is Mrs Cartwright.'

'I'll sit in on this if you don't mind, Jack. Bring her in Bateman,' said Murray as he put a third chair near to Jack's desk and sat down.

'I'm DI Riley and this is DCI Murray,' said Jack when the young woman came in. 'Please sit down, Mrs Cartwright.'

'Thank you.' The young woman sat opposite Jack, next to DCI Murray.

'What can I do for you?' Jack asked.

'I'm Rebecca Cartwright, formerly Rawlings. I used to work for the doctor as a nanny to Mark. Well, I mean Michael, but I knew him as Mark. I read in the paper that you wanted to speak to me.'

Murray gave Jack a stern look. 'Erm…yes I wanted to ask you about the Cartwright twins.'

'Jack!'

'Sir, I need to ask. I won't rest until I do.'

Murray sighed. 'Okay. Go ahead.'

'You were nanny to the boys?'

'No. I was nanny to Mark. David was looked after by his parents. He was favoured. I looked after Mark until he was six. His father's second cousin, James, used to visit often. We got to know each other and I married him three months after I left the doctor's employment. We didn't have any contact with them after the wedding. They're a funny lot. I'm divorced from James now, he was a womaniser, just like Matthew Cartwright.'

'How was Mark treated by his parents?'

'He wasn't loved, if that's what you mean. He wasn't wanted. I never saw any physical abuse, but the child was not happy. They were ashamed of him because of his deformity. As he got older he developed a kind of squint just below his right eye. I think it's called a tic. Whenever he got anxious or upset it would twitch uncontrollably until he'd calmed down.'

'Did his brother have the same facial tic?'

'Oh no. David was a happy confident child. He had whatever he wanted. They loved that one.'

'Well thank you for coming to see me, Mrs Cartwright.' Jack stood and shook her hand.

'I think I know why you wanted to see me, Inspector.'

'What do you think?'

'You think you have the wrong one, don't you?'

Jack's mouth dropped open. 'We have no evidence to think that, Mrs Cartwright.'

'Don't worry I'll say nothing to no-one.'

'Thank you.' Jack closed the door when she went out.

'Well? Come on. What's this all about?' Murray asked.

'I'd like to see the tapes of Steven Munroe's interview.'

'You think Mackenzie swapped places with him?'

'I don't know.'

'What if she's wrong and they both have a nervous tic?'

'I asked the nurses at the hospital. There's no sign of him having one. But Mrs Cartwright said it only appears when he's anxious, and he doesn't become anxious about anything.'

'What's your plan?'

'I don't have one. I'd like to look at the interview first.'

'I'll have a look with you.'

Jack got the interview up on one of the computers and he and Murray were watching it.

'Look. When I mentioned Rebecca his face twitched under his right eye.'

'I didn't see anything,' said Murray. 'Rewind it.'

Jack rewound the tape.

'Two tiny twitches,' said Murray. 'Then he put his hand on his cheek and scratched as if he had an itch. You can't say that's a tic, Jack, and you can't convict a man because his face twitched twice. I don't think it's enough for us to arrest him and I don't want to make the mistake and have the force sued for defamation of character and everything else his lawyers might throw at us. We need something more, Jack.'

'I might have something else, sir.'

Chapter Forty-Two

Two weeks later

It was a warm late August evening. Jack sat in the garden of Bumble Cottage and sipped a coke. Lily sat opposite him and cuddled a contented looking Daisy in her arms. He could hear her quiet murmur as she counted the baby's fingers and toes.

Her therapist said it would take a long time to get over the trauma of her kidnap ordeal at Tipley Manor. But all Jack could think was that he had her back and she talked and smiled a lot more now than she had when she first came home.

His mother and Kitty prepared food for the barbeque they were having to celebrate his forty-third birthday. Catherine had gone to visit her mother and would be back later. Sandy was still on leave and had gone to visit her mother in Manchester. She'd been asked to stay on at Dudstone for the foreseeable future, but Jack doubted she would stay long. She was destined for greater things within the force.

The cooler was stocked with drinks. He reflected

on the last two years of his life. They'd been the toughest he'd ever had to face. DCI Murray had given him a month off work to be with his family. He was tired, he needed a rest. No doubt he would get another call when the operation he and Murray had helped with was completed.

Constable Hadley lived in a semi-coma. There was not much hope that he would ever recover. Occasionally he opened his eyes and looked round the room. He couldn't speak or feed himself. Some of the Lost Girls and Mrs Cole had been found in the cellar at Tipley Manor. Bones and body parts were still being examined. It would take many months before the case could be closed.

The future looked good. His mother had softened towards him and Gwen was spending more time with him. The son who had known him as Uncle Jack accepted they had to get along for his mother's sake.

That morning he'd received a letter from the estate agents to inform him that his flats were sold and the contracts would be signed in six weeks. It was time to look for a new home for himself, Lily and Daisy. He was going to buy a big house so that his mother and Kitty could stay over. That's what he told them, but secretly he hoped that he and Gwen could get together and live there with their children.

Stella Baker's body had been released and yesterday he'd attended her funeral, along with Gwen, Lily and Ted Bateman. She had no living relatives and had left him a quarter of a million pounds, which he intended to spend wisely. His thoughts were interrupted when his mother called from the kitchen.

'Jack! Jack!'

He jumped up and ran into the house. 'What's the matter?'

His mother handed him her mobile phone. 'You'll have to go to Riley Cross, Jack. Fisheye's in trouble.'

'He's nothing but trouble!' said Jack. 'I'm going nowhere.'

'You must go, Jack! There's no-one else to help him. He's been accused of a terrible crime.'

'He's probably guilty then. All his life he's been nothing but a thief and a crook.'

'He's something else as well.'

'What? asked Jack.

'He's your father.'

Epilogue

Philip Clarke parked at the back of Segmore High Street. He waited for his date to show up. He wasn't sure whether she'd turn up or not. Sometimes girls said one thing, then did the opposite. She had sounded pretty certain though. She was late. He would wait another ten minutes, then go. He didn't want to attract attention to himself or his car, even though the number plate was false.

Segmore was a dopey kind of town. The folk seemed to walk about in a daze, or so he thought. The shops were closed, the street was empty, except for a couple of young boys who rode their bicycles round and round the car park. They were beginning to annoy him, but he knew if he said anything to them they would remember him, they might take his number. He didn't want them to remember him.

He kept his head slightly down as if he was looking at his phone or reading a newspaper.

She entered the car park from the bottom end by the shops and went to the bench and sat down. He wished the boys would just fuck off. They would see him approach her. He started the car and edged towards her. He looked in the mirror. The boys were behind him riding towards the exit. He stopped, opened the car door, got out and walked towards her.

'I'm Phil, Josh's brother,' he said. 'He's gutted he couldn't come himself, his leg is in plaster. You must be Emily.'

The girl turned her head to look at him.

A feeling of dread washed over him. It wasn't Emily. It was a young woman. Suddenly there were people running towards him from the back doors of the shops. It was a set up. The little bitch had told the police. Sirens blared and lights flashed as six police cars swooped on to the car park and surrounded him.

Operation Goldilocks was a success.

ABOUT THE AUTHOR

Jean was born and raised in the West Midlands. She has three children, ten grandchildren and three great grandchildren (soon to be five). Since leaving school she has gained a BA Hons in English and Women's Studies and an MA in the Teaching and Practice of Creative Writing. Jean lives close to her family in Dudley, West Midlands, UK.

Printed in Great Britain
by Amazon